VATHEK

LECTOR HOUSE PUBLIC DOMAIN WORKS

VATHEK

WILLIAM BECKFORD

ISBN: 978-93-5344-378-8

First Published: 1849

LECTOR HOUSE LLP
E-MAIL: lectorpublishing@gmail.com

VATHEK;

AN ARABIAN TALE,

BY

WILLIAM BECKFORD, ESQ.

WITH
NOTES, CRITICAL AND EXPLANATORY.

1849.

MEMOIR.
BY WILLIAM NORTH.

WILLIAM BECKFORD, the author of the following celebrated Eastern tale, was born in 1760, and died in the spring of 1844, at the advanced age of eighty-four years. It is to be regretted, that a man of so remarkable a character, did not leave the world some record of a life offering points of interest different from that of any of his contemporaries, from the peculiarly studious retirement and eccentric avocations in which it was chiefly passed. Such a memoir would have formed a curious contrast with that of the late M. de Chateaubriand, who, born nearly at the same period, outlived but by a few years, the strange Englishman, whose famous romance forms a brilliant ornament to French literature, which even Atala is unlikely to outlive in the memory of Chateaubriand's countrymen. All men of genius should write autobiographies. Such works are inestimable lessons to posterity. As it is, there are few men, of whom it is more difficult to compose an elaborate and detailed history than the author of "Vathek." From such scanty sources as are open to us, the reader must be content with a few striking facts and illustrations, which may serve to convey some idea of the idiosyncrasy of a man, whose whole life was a sort of mystery, even to his personal acquaintances.

His great-great-grandfather was lieutenant-governor and commander of the forces in Jamaica; and his grandfather president of the council in the same island. His father, though not a merchant, as has been represented, but a large landed proprietor, both in England and the West Indies, was lord mayor of London, and distinguished himself in presenting an address to the king, George the Third,—by a spirited retort to his majesty,—who had the ill-breeding to treat discourteously a deputation which the lord mayor headed. The portraits of Alderman Beckford, and his more celebrated son, were painted by Sir Joshua Reynolds. The former died in 1770, leaving the subject of this memoir the wealthiest commoner in England.

No pains were spared on the education of the young Croesus—the lords Chatham and Camden being consulted by his father on that subject. Besides Latin and Greek, he spoke five modern languages, and wrote three with facility and elegance. He read Persian and Arabic, designed with great skill, and studied the science of music under the great Mozart.

At the age of eighteen he visited Paris, and was introduced to Voltaire. "On taking leave of me," said Beckford, "he placed his hand on my head, saying, 'There, young Englishman, I give you the blessing of a very old man.' Voltaire was a mere skeleton—a bony anatomy. His countenance I shall never forget."

His first literary production, "Memoirs of Extraordinary Painters," was written at the early age of seventeen. It would appear, that the old housekeeper at Fonthill, was in the habit of edifying visitors to its picture gallery by a description of the paintings, mainly derived from her own fertile imagination. This suggested to our author, the humorous idea of composing a catalogue of supposititious painters with histories of each, equally fanciful and grotesque. Henceforward, the old housekeeper had a printed guide (or rather, mis-guider) to go by, and could discourse at large on the merits of Og of Bashan! Waterslouchy of Amsterdam! and Herr Sucrewasser of Vienna! their wives and styles! As for the country squires, etc., "they," Beckford tells us, "took all for gospel."

"Vathek,"—the superb "Vathek," which Lord Byron so much admired, and on which he so frequently complimented the author,—"Vathek," the finest of Oriental romances, as "Lallah Rookh" is the first of Oriental poems, by the pen of a "Frank," was written and published before our author had completed his twentieth year, it having been composed at a *single sitting*! Yes, for three days and two nights did the indefatigable author persevere in his task. He completed it, and a serious illness was the result. What other literary man ever equalled this feat of rapidity and genius?

"Vathek" was originally written in French, of which its style is a model. The translation which follows, is not by the author himself, though he expressed perfect satisfaction with it. It was originally published in 1786. For splendour of description, exquisite humour, and supernatural interest and grandeur, it stands without a rival in romance. In as thoroughly Oriental keeping, Hope's "Anastasius, or Memoirs of a Modern Greek," which Beckford himself highly admired, can alone be compared with it.

Much of the description of Vathek's palace, and even the renowned "Hall of Eblis," was afterwards visibly embodied in the real Fonthill Abbey, of which wonders, almost as fabulous, were at one time reported and believed.

Fonthill Abbey, which had been destroyed by fire, and re-built during the lifetime of the elder Beckford, was on account of its bad site demolished, and again re-built under the superintendence of our author himself, assisted by James Wyatt, Esq., the architect, with a magnificence that excited the greatest attention and wonder at the time. The total outlay of building Fonthill, including furniture, articles of virtu, etc., must have been enormous, not much within the million, as estimated by the "Times." A writer in the "Athenæum" mentions £400,000 as the sum. Beckford informed Mr. Cyrus Redding, that the exact cost of building Fonthill was £273,000.

The distinguishing architectural peculiarity of Fonthill Abbey, was a lofty tower, 280 feet in height. This tower was prominently shadowed forth in "Vathek," and shows how strong a hold the idea had upon his mind. Such was his impatience to see Fonthill completed, that he had the works continued by torchlight, with relays of workmen. During the progress of the building, the tower caught fire, and was partly destroyed. The owner, however, was present, and enjoyed the magnificent burning spectacle. It was soon restored; but a radical fault in laying the foundation, caused it eventually to fall down, and leave Fonthill a ruin in the life-time of its founder.

Not so much his extravagant mode of life, which is the common notion, as the loss of two large estates in a law suit (the value of which may be inferred from the fact, that *fifteen hundred slaves* were upon them) induced our author to quit Fonthill, and offer it and its contents for public sale. There was a general desire to see the interior of the palace, in which its lord had lived in a luxurious seclusion, so little admired by the curious of the fashionable world. "He is fortunate," says the "Times" of 1822, "who finds a vacant chair within twenty miles of Fonthill; the solitude of a private apartment is a luxury which few can hope for." . . . "Falstaff himself could not *take his ease* at this moment within a dozen leagues of Fonthill." . . . "The beds through the county are (literally) doing double duty—people who come in from a distance during the night must wait to go to bed until others get up in the morning." . . . "Not a farm-house, however humble,—not a cottage near Fonthill, but gives shelter to fashion, to beauty, and rank; ostrich plumes, which, by their very waving, we can trace back to Piccadilly, are seen nodding at a casement window over a depopulated poultry-yard."

The costly treasures of art and virtu, as well as the furniture of the rich mansion, were scattered far and wide; and one of its tables served the writer of this memoir to scribble upon, when first stern necessity, or yet sterner ambition, urged him to add his mite to the Babel tower of literature. At that table I first read "Vathek." I have read it often since, and every perusal has increased my admiration.

Nearly fifty years after the publication of "Vathek," in 1835, Mr. Beckford published his "Recollections of an Excursion to the Monasteries of Alcobaca and Batalha," which he had taken in 1795, together with an epistolatory record of his observations in Italy, Spain and Portugal, between the years 1780 and 1794. These are marked, as he himself intimates, "with the bloom and heyday of youthful spirits and youthful confidence, at a period when the older order of things existed with all its picturesque pomps and absurdities; when Venice enjoyed her Piombi and sub-marine dungeons; Prance her Bastille; the Peninsula her Holy Inquisition." With none of those subjects, however, are the letters occupied—but with delineations of landscape, and the effects of natural phenomena. These literary efforts appear to have exhausted their author's productive powers; in a word, he seems soon to have been "used-up," and then to have discontinued his search after new sensations, or to have been content to live without them.

After the sale of Fonthill, our author lived a considerable time in Portugal, and hence Lord Byron, who was fond of casting the shadow of his own imagination over every object, penned the well-known lines at Cintra:

> "There thou, too, Vathek, England's wealthiest son,
> Once formed thy paradise; as not aware
> Where wanton wealth her mightiest deeds hath done,
> Meek peace, voluptuous lures, was ever wont to shun.
>
> Here didst thou dwell; here scenes of pleasure plan,
> Beneath yon mountain's ever beauteous brow;
> But now, as if a thing unblest by man,

Thy fairy dwelling is as lone as thou!
Here giant weeds a passage scarce allow
To halls deserted; portals gaping wide
Fresh lessons to the thinking bosom; how
Vain are the pleasaunces on earth supplied,
Swept into wrecks anon by time's ungentle tide."

These sombre verses contrast strangely with Beckford's saying to Mr. Cyrus Redding, in his seventy-sixth year, "that he had never felt a moments' ennui in his life."

Beckford was in person scarcely above the middle height, slender, and well formed, with features indicating great intellectual power. He was exactly one year younger than Pitt, the companion of his minority. His political principles were popular, though it is recorded, that at a court ball on the Queen's birth-day, in 1782, he, with Miss North, led up a country dance. He sat in parliament, in his early years, both for Wells and Hendon, but retired on account of bad health. This, however, he overcame by careful diet and exercise, as testified by his great bodily activity almost to the last. He was a man of most extensive reading, and cultivated taste.

The last years of his life were passed at Bath—where he united two houses in Lansdown Crescent, by an arch thrown across the street, and containing his library, which was well selected, and very extensive. Not far off, he again erected a tower, 180 feet high, of which the following description was given at the time of his decease, by a correspondent of the Athenæum:—

"Mr. Beckford, at an early period of his residence there, erected a lofty tower, in the apartments of which were placed many of his choicest paintings and articles of virtu. Asiatic in its style, with gilded lattices and blinds, or curtains, of crimson cloth, its striped ceilings, its minaret, and other accessories, conveyed the idea that the being who designed the place and endeavoured to carry out the plan, was deeply imbued with the spirit of that lonely grandeur and strict solitariness which obtains through all countries and among all people of the East. The building was surrounded by a high wall, and entrance afforded to the garden in which the tower stood, by a door of small dimensions. The garden itself was Eastern in its character. Though comparatively circumscribed in its size, nevertheless were to be found within it, solitary walks and deep retiring shades, such as could be supposed Vathek, the mournful and the magnificent, loved, and from the bowers of which might be expected would suddenly fall upon the ear, sounds of the cymbal and the dulcimer. The building contained several apartments crowded with the finest paintings. At the time I made my inspection the walls were crowded with the choicest productions of the easel. The memory falls back upon ineffaceable impressions of Old Franks, Breughel, Cuyp, Titian, (a Holy Family), Hondekooter, Polemberg, and a host of other painters whose works have immortalized Art. Ornaments of the most exquisite gold fillagree, carvings in ivory and wood, Raphaelesque china, goblets formed of gems, others fashioned by the miraculous hands of Benvenuto Cellini, filled the many cabinets and *recherché* receptacles created for such things. The doors of the rooms were of finely polished wood—the windows of single sweeps of plate glass—the cornices of gilded silver; every part, both within and without, bespeaking the wealth, the magnificence, and the taste of him who had built this temple in dedication to grandeur, solitariness, and the arts."

From the summit of this tower, Mr. Beckford, and he alone without a telescope,—could behold that other tower of his youthful magnificence, Fonthill; on which he loved to gaze, with feelings which it would be difficult to describe. His eyesight was wonderful; he could gaze upon the sun like an eagle; and on the day that the great tower at Fonthill fell he missed it in the landscape long before the news of the catastrophe reached Bath.

In conclusion, we have only to add, that our author, in his life-time, had all that wealth can give, and in his grave his memory will retain that which no wealth can purchase. Whatever may have been his errors, they have died with him. His genius yet lives, and "Vathek," now for the first time presented to the public in a popular form, will, whilst English literature lasts, never want readers, and, while good taste flourishes, admirers.

PREFACE.

The original of the following story, with some others of a similar kind, collected in the east by a man of letters, was communicated to the editor above three years ago. The pleasure he received from the perusal of it induced him at that time to transcribe, and since to translate it. How far the copy may be a just representation it becomes not him to determine. He presumes however to hope that if the difficulty of accommodating our English idioms to the Arabic, preserving the correspondent tones of a diversified narration, and discriminating the nicer touches of character through the shades of foreign manners be duly considered, a failure in some points will not preclude him from all claim to indulgence; especially if those images, sentiments, and passions, which being independent of local peculiarities, may be expressed in every language, shall be found to retain their native energy in our own.

VATHEK.

VATHEK, ninth Caliph[1] of the race of the Abassides, was the son of Motassem, and the grandson of Haroun Al Raschid. From an early accession to the throne, and the talents he possessed to adorn it, his subjects were induced to expect that his reign would be long and happy. His figure was pleasing and majestic; but when he was angry, one of his eyes became so terrible[2] that no person could bear to behold it; and the wretch upon whom it was fixed instantly fell backward, and sometimes expired. For fear, however, of depopulating his dominions, and making his palace desolate, he but rarely gave way to his anger.

Being much addicted to women, and the pleasures of the table, he sought by his affability to procure agreeable companions; and he succeeded the better, as his generosity was unbounded and his indulgences unrestrained; for he was by no means scrupulous: nor did he think, with the Caliph Omar Ben Abdalaziz,[3] that it was necessary to make a hell of this world to enjoy Paradise in the next.

He surpassed in magnificence all his predecessors. The palace of Alkoremmi, which his father Motassem had erected on the hill of Pied Horses, and which commanded the whole city of Samarah,[4] was in his idea far too scanty: he added, therefore, five wings, or rather other palaces, which he destined for the particular gratification of each of his senses.

In the first of these were tables continually covered with the most exquisite

---

[1] *Caliph.* This title amongst the Mahometans comprehends the concrete character of prophet, priest, and king; and is used to signify *the Vicar of God on earth.*—Habesci's State of the Ottoman Empire, p. 9. Herbelot, p. 985.

[2] *One of his eyes became so terrible.* The author of Nighiaristan hath preserved a fact that supports this account; and there is no history of Vathek, in which his *terrible eye* is not mentioned.

[3] *Omar Ben Abdalaziz.* This Caliph was eminent above all others for temperance and self-denial; insomuch, that he is believed to have been raised to Mahomet's bosom, as a reward for his abstinence in an age of corruption. Herbelot, p. 690.

[4] *Samarah.* A city of the Babylonian Irak, supposed to have stood on the site where Nimrod erected his tower. Khondemir relates, in his life of Motassem, that this prince, to terminate the disputes which were perpetually happening between the inhabitants of Bagdat and his Turkish slaves, withdrew from thence; and, having fixed on a situation in the plain of Catoul, there founded Samarah. He is said to have had in the stables of this city a hundred and thirty thousand pied horses; each of which carried, by his order, a sack of earth to a place he had chosen. By this accumulation, an elevation was formed that commanded a view of all Samarah, and served for the foundation of his magnificent palace. Herbelot, p. 752, 808, 985. Anecdotes Arabes, p. 413.

dainties, which were supplied both by night and by day according to their constant consumption; whilst the most delicious wines, and the choicest cordials, flowed forth from a hundred fountains, that were never exhausted. This palace was called "The Eternal, or Unsatiating Banquet."

The second was styled "The Temple of Melody, or the Nectar of the Soul." It was inhabited by the most skilful musicians and admired poets of the time, who not only displayed their talents within, but dispersing in bands without, caused every surrounding scene to reverberate their songs, which were continually varied in the most delightful succession.

The palace named "The Delight of the Eyes, or the Support of Memory," was one entire enchantment. Rarities collected from every corner of the earth were there found in such profusion as to dazzle and confound, but for the order in which they were arranged. One gallery exhibited the pictures of the celebrated Mani; and statues that seemed to be alive. Here a well-managed perspective attracted the sight; there, the magic of optics agreeably deceived it; whilst the naturalist, on his part, exhibited in their several classes the various gifts that heaven had bestowed on our globe. In a word, Vathek omitted nothing in this particular that might gratify the curiosity of those who resorted to it, although he was not able to satisfy his own; for he was, of all men, the most curious.

"The Palace of Perfumes," which was termed likewise, "The Incentive to Pleasure," consisted of various halls, where the different perfumes which the earth produces were kept perpetually burning in censers of gold. Flambeaus and aromatic lamps were here lighted in open day; but the too powerful effects of this agreeable delirium might be avoided by descending into an immense garden, where an assemblage of every fragrant flower diffused through the air the purest odours.

The fifth palace, denominated "The Retreat of Joy, or the Dangerous," was frequented by troops of young females, beautiful as the Houris,[5] and not less seducing, who never failed to receive with caresses all whom the Caliph allowed to approach them; for he was by no means disposed to be jealous, as his own women were secluded within the palace he inhabited himself.

Notwithstanding the sensuality in which Vathek indulged, he experienced no abatement in the love of his people, who thought that a sovereign immersed in pleasure was not less tolerable to his subjects than one that employed himself in creating them foes. But the unquiet and impetuous disposition of the Caliph would not allow him to rest there: he had studied so much for his amusement in the life-time of his father as to acquire a great deal of knowledge, though not a sufficiency to satisfy himself; for he wished to know everything; even sciences that did not exist. He was fond of engaging in disputes with the learned, but liked them not to push their opposition with warmth. He stopped the mouths of those <u>with presents, w</u>hose mouths could be stopped; whilst others, whom his liberality

[5] *Houris.* The Virgins of Paradise, called, from their large black eyes, *Hur al oyun.* An intercourse with these, according to the institution of Mahomet, is to constitute the principal felicity of the faithful. Not formed of clay, like mortal women, they are deemed in the highest degree beautiful, and exempt from every inconvenience incident to the sex. Al Koran; passim.

was unable to subdue, he sent to prison to cool their blood; a remedy that often succeeded.

Vathek discovered also a predilection for theological controversy; but it was not with the orthodox that he usually held. By this means he induced the zealots to oppose him, and then persecuted them in return; for he resolved, at any rate, to have reason on his side.

The great prophet Mahomet, whose vicars the Caliphs are, beheld with indignation from his abode in the seventh heaven the irreligious conduct of such a vicegerent.

"Let us leave him to himself," said he to the Genii,[6] who are always ready to receive his commands; "let us see to what lengths his folly and impiety will carry him; if he run into excess we shall know how to chastise him. Assist him, therefore, to complete the tower which, in imitation of Nimrod, he hath begun; not, like that great warrior, to escape being drowned, but from the insolent curiosity of penetrating the secrets of heaven: he will not divine the fate that awaits him."

The Genii obeyed; and when the workmen had raised their structure a cubit in the day time, two cubits more were added in the night. The expedition with which the fabric arose was not a little flattering to the vanity of Vathek. He fancied that even insensible matter showed forwardness to subserve his designs; not considering that the successes of the foolish and wicked form the first rod of their chastisement.

His pride arrived at its height when, having ascended, for the first time, the eleven thousand stairs of his tower, he cast his eyes below and beheld men not larger than pismires; mountains than shells; and cities than bee-hives. The idea which such an elevation inspired of his own grandeur completely bewildered him; he was almost ready to adore himself; till lifting his eyes upwards, he saw the stars as high above him as they appeared when he stood on the surface of the earth. He consoled himself, however, for this transient perception of his littleness with the thought of being great in the eyes of the others, and flattered himself that the light of his mind would extend beyond the reach of his sight, and transfer to the stars the decrees of his destiny.

With this view the inquisitive prince passed most of his nights on the summit of his tower, till he became an adept in the mysteries of astrology, and imagined that the planets had disclosed to him the most marvellous adventures, which were to be accomplished by an extraordinary personage, from a country altogether unknown. Prompted by motives of curiosity, he had always been courteous to strangers; but from this instant he redoubled his attention, and ordered it to be

---

[6] *Genii.* Genn or Ginn, in the Arabic, signifies a Genius or Demon — a being of a higher order, and formed of more subtile matter than man. According to Oriental mythology, the Genii governed the world long before the creation of Adam. The Mahometans regarded them as an intermediate race between angels and men, and capable of salvation: whence Mahomet pretended a commission to convert them. Consonant to this, we read that, "When the servant of God stood up to invoke him, it wanted little but that the Genii had pressed on him in crowds, to hear him rehearse the Koran." Herbelot, p. 357. Al Koran ch. 72.

announced by sound of trumpet, through all the streets of Samarah, that no one of his subjects, on peril of his displeasure, should either lodge or detain a traveller, but forthwith bring him to the palace.

Not long after this proclamation, there arrived in his metropolis, a man so hideous that the very guards who arrested him were forced to shut their eyes as they led him along. The Caliph himself appeared startled at so horrible a visage; but joy succeeded to this emotion of terror when the stranger displayed to his view such rarities as he had never before seen, and of which he had no conception.

In reality, nothing was ever so extraordinary as the merchandise this stranger produced. Most of his curiosities, which were not less admirable for their workmanship than their splendour, had besides, their several virtues described on a parchment fastened to each. There were slippers which enabled the feet to walk; knives that cut without the motion of a hand; sabres which dealt the blow at the person they were wished to strike; and the whole enriched with gems that were hitherto unknown.

The sabres, whose blades emitted a dazzling radiance, fixed more than all the Caliph's attention, who promised himself to decipher at his leisure the uncouth characters engraven on their sides. Without, therefore, demanding their price, he ordered all the coined gold to be brought from his treasury, and commanded the merchant to take what he pleased. The stranger complied with modesty and silence.

Vathek, imagining that the merchant's taciturnity was occasioned by the awe which his presence inspired, encouraged him to advance, and asked him, with an air of condescension, "Who he was? whence he came? and where he obtained such beautiful commodities?"

The man, or rather monster, instead of making a reply, thrice rubbed his forehead, which, as well as his body, was blacker than ebony; four times clapped his paunch, the projection of which was enormous; opened wide his huge eyes, which glowed like firebrands; began to laugh with a hideous noise, and discovered his long amber coloured teeth bestreaked with green.

The Caliph, though a little startled, renewed his enquiries, but without being able to procure a reply. At which, beginning to be ruffled, he exclaimed, "knowest thou, varlet, who I am? and at whom thou art aiming thy gibes?" Then addressing his guards, "have ye heard him speak? is he dumb?"

"He hath spoken," they replied, "though but little."

"Let him speak then again," said Vathek, "and tell me who he is, from whence he came, and where he procured these singular curiosities, or I swear, by the ass of Balaam, that I will make him rue his pertinacity."

This menace was accompanied by the Caliph with one of his angry and perilous glances, which the stranger sustained without the slightest emotion, although his eyes were fixed on the terrible eye of the prince.

No words can describe the amazement of the courtiers, when they beheld this rude merchant withstand the encounter unshocked. They all fell prostrate with their faces on the ground, to avoid the risk of their lives, and continued in the same abject posture till the Caliph exclaimed in a furious tone:

"Up, cowards! seize the miscreant! see that he be committed to prison, and guarded by the best of my soldiers! Let him, however, retain the money I gave him; it is not my intent to take from him his property, I only want him to speak."

No sooner had he uttered these words than the stranger was surrounded, pinioned with strong fetters, and hurried away to the prison of the great tower, which was encompassed by seven empalements of iron bars, and armed with spikes in every direction, longer and sharper than spits.

The Caliph, nevertheless, remained in the most violent agitation. He sat down indeed to eat, but of the three hundred covers that were daily placed before him, could taste of no more than thirty-two.

A diet to which he had been so little accustomed, was sufficient of itself to prevent him from sleeping, what then must be its effect when joined to the anxiety that prayed upon his spirits? At the first glimpse of dawn he hastened to the prison, again to importune this intractable stranger; but the rage of Vathek exceeded all bounds on finding the prison empty, the gates burst asunder, and his guards lying lifeless around him. In the paroxysm of his passion he fell furiously on the poor carcases, and kicked them till evening without intermission. His courtiers and viziers exerted their efforts to soothe his extravagance, but finding every expedient ineffectual, they all united in one vociferation:

"The Caliph is gone mad! the Caliph is out of his senses!"

This outcry, which was soon resounded through the streets of Samarah, at length reached the ears of Carathis, his mother: she flew in the utmost consternation to try her ascendency on the mind of her son. Her tears and caresses called off his attention; and he was prevailed upon by her entreaties to be brought back to the palace.

Carathis, apprehensive of leaving Vathek to himself, caused him to be put to bed; and seating herself by him, endeavoured by her conversation to heal and compose him. Nor could any one have attempted it with better success; for the Caliph not only loved her as a mother but respected her as a person of superior genius. It was she who had induced him, being a Greek herself, to adopt all the sciences and systems of her country, which good Mussulmans hold in such thorough abhorrence.

Judicial astrology was one of those systems in which Carathis was a perfect adept. She began, therefore, with reminding her son of the promise which the stars had made him; and intimated an intention of consulting them again.

"Alas!" sighed the Caliph, as soon at he could speak, "what a fool have I been! not for the kicks bestowed on my guards, who so tamely submitted to death, but for never considering that this extraordinary man was the same the planets had foretold; whom, instead of ill-treating, I should have conciliated by all the arts of persuasion."

"The past," said Carathis, "cannot be recalled; but it behoves us to think of the future: perhaps you may again see the object you so much regret: it is possible the inscriptions on the sabres will afford information. Eat, therefore, and take thy repose, my dear son. We will consider, to-morrow, in what manner to act."

Vathek yielded to her counsel as well as he could, and arose in the morning with a mind more at ease. The sabres he commanded to be instantly brought; and poring upon them through a green glass, that their glittering might not dazzle, he set himself in earnest to decipher the inscriptions; but his reiterated attempts were all of them nugatory: in vain did he beat his head and bite his nails; not a letter of the whole was he able to ascertain. So unlucky a disappointment would have undone him again, had not Carathis, by good fortune, entered the apartment.

"Have patience, son!" said she. "You certainly are possessed of every important science, but the knowledge of languages is a trifle, at best; and the accomplishment of none but a pedant. Issue forth a proclamation that you will confer such rewards as become your greatness upon any one that shall interpret what you do not understand, and what it is beneath you to learn. You will soon find your curiosity gratified."

"That may be," said the Caliph; "but in the mean time I shall be horribly disgusted by a crowd of smatterers, who will come to the trial as much for the pleasure of retailing their jargon as from the hope of gaining the reward. To avoid this evil, it will be proper to add that I will put every candidate to death who shall fail to give satisfaction; for, thank heaven, I have skill enough to distinguish between one that translates and one that invents."

"Of that I have no doubt," replied Carathis, "but to put the ignorant to death is somewhat severe, and may be productive of dangerous effects. Content yourself with commanding their beards to be burnt: beards, in a state, are not quite so essential as men."

The Caliph submitted to the reasons of his mother, and sending for Morakanabad, his prime vizier, said:

"Let the common criers proclaim, not only in Samarah, but throughout every city in my empire, that whosoever will repair hither, and decipher certain characters which appear to be inexplicable, shall experience the liberality for which I am renowned; but that all who fail upon trial shall have their beards burnt off to the last hair. Let them add also, that I will bestow fifty beautiful slaves, and as many jars of apricots from the isle of Kirmith, upon any man that shall bring me intelligence of the stranger."

The subjects of the Caliph, like their sovereign, being great admirers of women, and apricots from Kirmith, felt their mouths water at these promises, but were totally unable to gratify their hankering, for no one knew which way the stranger had gone.

As to the Caliph's other requisition the result was different: the learned, the half-learned, and those who were neither, but fancied themselves equal to both, came boldly to hazard their beards, and all shamefully lost them.

The exaction of these forfeitures, which found sufficient employment for the

Eunuchs, gave them such a smell of singed hair as greatly to disgust the ladies of the seraglio, and make it necessary that this new occupation of their guardians should be transferred into other hands.

At length, however, an old man presented himself, whose beard was a cubit-and-a-half longer than any that had appeared before him. The officers of the palace whispered to each other, as they ushered him in:

"What a pity such a beard should be burnt!"

Even the Caliph, when he saw it, concurred with them in opinion; but his concern was entirely needless. This venerable personage read the characters with facility, and explained them verbatim, as follows:

"We were made where everything good is made; we are the least of the wonders of a place where all is wonderful; and deserving the sight of the first potentate on earth."

"You translate admirably!" cried Vathek. "I know to what these marvellous characters allude. Let him receive as many robes of honour, and thousands of sequins of gold, as he hath spoken words. I am in some measure relieved from the perplexity that embarrassed me!"

Vathek invited the old man to dine, and even to remain some days in the palace. Unluckily for him, he accepted the offer; for the Caliph having ordered him next morning to be called, said:

"Read again to me what you have read already; I cannot hear too often the promise that is made me, the completion of which I languish to obtain."

The old man forthwith put on his green spectacles; but they instantly dropped from his nose, on perceiving that the characters he had read the day preceding, had given place to others of different import.

"What ails you?" asked the Caliph; "and why these symptoms of wonder?"

"Sovereign of the world," replied the old man, "these sabres hold another language to-day, from that they yesterday held."

"How say you?" returned Vathek. "But it matters not! tell me, if you can, what they mean."

"It is this, my lord," rejoined the old man: "'Woe to the rash mortal who seeks to know that of which he should remain ignorant and to undertake that which surpasseth his power!'"

"And woe to thee!" cried the Caliph, in a burst of indignation: "to-day thou art void of understanding: begone from my presence, they shall burn but the half of thy beard, because thou wert yesterday fortunate in guessing. My gifts I never resume."

The old man, wise enough to perceive he had luckily escaped, considering the folly of disclosing so disgusting a truth, immediately withdrew, and appeared not again.

But it was not long before Vathek discovered abundant reason to regret his precipitation; for though he could not decipher the characters himself, yet, by constantly poring upon them, he plainly perceived that they every day changed; and unfortunately no other candidate offered to explain them. This perplexing occupation inflamed his blood, dazzled his sight, and brought on a giddiness and debility that he could not support. He failed not, however, though in so reduced a condition, to be often carried to his tower, as he flattered himself that he might there read in the stars, which he went to consult, something more congruous to his wishes. But in this his hopes were deluded; for his eyes, dimmed by the vapours of his head, began to subserve his curiosity so ill, that he beheld nothing but a thick dun cloud, which he took for the most direful of omens.

Agitated with so much anxiety, Vathek entirely lost all firmness; a fever seized him and his appetite failed. Instead of being one of the greatest eaters, he became as distinguished for drinking. So insatiable was the thirst which tormented him, that his mouth, like a funnel, was always open to receive the various liquors that might be poured into it and especially cold water, which calmed him more than every other.

This unhappy prince being thus incapacitated for the enjoyment of any pleasure, commanded the palaces of the five senses to be shut up; forebore to appear in public, either to display his magnificence or administer justice; and retired to the inmost apartment of his harem. As he had ever been an indulgent husband, his wives, overwhelmed with grief at his deplorable situation, incessantly offered their prayers for his health, and unremittingly supplied him with water.

In the mean time, the Princess Carathis, whose affliction no words can describe, instead of restraining herself to sobbing and tears, was closeted daily with the Vizier Morakanabad, to find out some cure or mitigation of the Caliph's disease. Under the persuasion that it was caused by enchantment, they turned over together leaf by leaf, all the books of magic that might point out a remedy; and caused the horrible stranger, whom they accused as the enchanter, to be everywhere sought for with the strictest diligence.

At the distance of a few miles from Samarah stood a high mountain, whose sides were swarded with wild thyme and basil, and its summit overspread with so delightful a plain that it might be taken for the Paradise destined for the faithful. Upon it grew a hundred thickets of eglantine and other fragrant shrubs; a hundred arbours of roses, jessamine, and honeysuckle; as many clumps of orange trees, cedar, and citron; whose branches, interwoven with the palm, the pomegranate, and the vine, presented every luxury that could regale the eye or the taste. The ground was strewed with violets, harebells, and pansies; in the midst of which sprung forth tufts of jonquils, hyacinths, and carnations, with every other perfume that impregnates the air. Four fountains, not less clear than deep, and so abundant as to slake the thirst of ten armies, seemed purposely placed here to make the scene more resemble the garden of Eden, which was watered by the four sacred rivers. Here the nightingale sang the birth of the rose, her well-beloved, and at the same time lamented its short-lived beauty; whilst the turtle deplored the loss of more substantial pleasures and the wakeful lark hailed the rising light that reanimates the whole creation. Here, more than anywhere, the mingled melodies of birds expressed the various passions they inspired; as if the exquisite fruits, which they pecked at pleasure, had given them a double energy.

To this mountain Vathek was sometimes brought, for the sake of breathing a purer air; and especially, to drink at will of the four fountains, which were reputed in the highest degree salubrious, and sacred to himself. His attendants were his mother, his wives, and some eunuchs, who assiduously employed themselves in filling capacious bowls of rock crystal, and emulously presenting them to him. But it frequently happened that his avidity exceeded their zeal; insomuch that he would prostrate himself upon the ground to lap up the water, of which he could never have enough.

One day when this unhappy prince had been long lying in so debasing a posture, a voice, hoarse but strong, thus addressed him:

"Why assumest thou the function of a dog, oh Caliph, so proud of thy dignity and power?"

At this apostrophe he raised up his head and beheld the stranger that had caused him so much affliction. Inflamed with anger at the sight, he exclaimed:

"Accursed Giaour![7] what comest thou hither to do? is it not enough to have transformed a prince, remarkable for his agility, into one of those leather barrels which the Bedouin Arabs carry on their camels when they traverse the deserts? Perceivest thou not that I may perish by drinking to excess, no less than by a total abstinence?"

"Drink then this draught," said the stranger, as he presented to him a phial of a red and yellow mixture; "and to satiate the thirst of thy soul as well as of thy body, know that I am an Indian, but from a region of India which is wholly unknown."

The Caliph, delighted to see his desires accomplished in part, and flattering himself with the hope of obtaining their entire fulfilment, without a moment's hesitation swallowed the potion, and instantaneously found his health restored, his thirst appeased, and his limbs as agile as ever.

In the transports of his joy, Vathek leaped upon the neck of the frightful Indian, and kissed his horrid mouth and hollow cheeks, as though they had been the coral lips, and the lilies and roses of his most beautiful wives; whilst they, less terrified than jealous at the sight, dropped their veils to hide the blush of mortification that suffused their foreheads.

Nor would the scene have closed here, had not Carathis, with all the art of insinuation, a little repressed the raptures of her son. Having prevailed upon him to return to Samarah, she caused a herald to precede him, whom she commanded to proclaim as loudly as possible:

"The wonderful stranger hath appeared again; he hath healed the Caliph; he hath spoken! he hath spoken!"

[7] *Accursed Giaour*. Dives of this kind are frequently mentioned by Eastern writers. Consult their tales in general, and especially those of "The Fisherman," "Aladdin," and "The Princess of China."

Forthwith all the inhabitants of this vast city quitted their habitations, and ran together in crowds to see the procession of Vathek and the Indian, whom they now blessed as much as they had before execrated, incessantly shouting,

"He hath healed our sovereign; he hath spoken! he hath spoken!"

Nor were these words forgotten in the public festivals, which were celebrated the same evening to testify the general joy, for the poets applied them as a chorus to all the songs they composed.

The Caliph, in the mean while caused the palaces of the senses to be again set open, and as he found himself prompted to visit that of taste, in preference to the rest, immediately ordered a splendid entertainment, to which his great officers and favourite courtiers were all invited. The Indian, who was placed near the prince, seemed to think that as a proper acknowledgment of so distinguished a privilege, he could neither eat, drink, nor talk too much. The various dainties were no sooner served up than they vanished, to the great mortification of Vathek, who piqued himself on being the greatest eater alive, and at this time in particular had an excellent appetite.

The rest of the company looked round at each other in amazement, but the Indian without appearing to observe it, quaffed large bumpers to the health of each of them: sung in a style altogether extravagant; related stories at which he laughed immoderately; and poured forth extemporaneous verses which would not have been thought bad, but for the strange grimaces with which they were uttered. In a word, his loquacity was equal to that of a hundred astrologers; he ate as much as a hundred porters, and caroused in proportion.

The Caliph, notwithstanding the table had been thirty times covered, found himself incommoded by the voraciousness of his guest, who was now considerably declined in the prince's esteem. Vathek, however, being unwilling to betray the chagrin he could hardly disguise, said in a whisper to Bababalouk,[8] the chief of his eunuchs:

"You see how enormous his performances in every way are; what would be the consequence should he get at my wives? Go! redouble your vigilance, and be sure look well to my Circassians, who would be more to his taste than all of the rest."

The bird of the morning had thrice renewed his song, when the hour of the divan[9] sounded. Vathek, in gratitude to his subjects, having promised to attend, immediately arose from table and repaired thither leaning upon his vizier, who could scarcely support him, so disordered was the poor prince by the wine he had drank, and still more by the extravagant vagaries of his boisterous guest.

---

[8] *Bababalouk, the Chief of his Eunuchs.* As it was the employment of the black eunuchs to wait upon, and guard the sultanas, to the general superintendence of the Harem was particularly committed to their chief. Habesci's State of the Ottoman Empire, p. 155–6.

[9] *The Divan.* This was both the supreme council, and court of justice, at which the Caliphs of the race of the Abassides assisted in person to redress the injuries of every appellant. Herbelot, p. 298.

The viziers, the officers of the crown, and of the law, arranged themselves in a semi-circle about their sovereign, and preserved a respectful silence, whilst the Indian, who looked as cool as if come from a fast, sat down without ceremony on a step of the throne, laughing in his sleeve at the indignation with which his temerity had filled the spectators.

The Caliph, however, whose ideas were confused and his head embarrassed, went on administering justice at hap-hazard, till at length the prime vizier[10] perceiving his situation, hit upon a sudden expedient to interrupt the audience, and rescue the honour of his master, to whom he said in a whisper:

"My lord, the princess Carathis, who hath passed the night in consulting the planets, informs you that they portend you evil; and the danger is urgent. Beware, lest this stranger whom you have so lavishly recompensed for his magical gewgaws, should make some attempt on your life: his liquor, which at first had the appearance of effecting your cure, may be no more than a poison of a sudden operation. Slight not this surmise; ask him, at least, of what it was compounded; whence he procured it; and mention the sabres, which you seem to have forgotten."

Vathek, to whom the insolent airs of the stranger became every moment less supportable, intimated to his vizier by a wink of acquiescence, that he would adopt his advice, and at once turning towards the Indian, said:

"Get up and declare in full divan of what drugs the liquor was compounded you enjoined me to take, for it is suspected to be poison; add also the explanation I have so earnestly desired concerning the sabres you sold me, and thus show your gratitude for the favours heaped on you."

Having pronounced these words in as moderate a tone as a Caliph well could, he waited in silent expectation for an answer; but the Indian, still keeping his seat, began to renew his loud shouts of laughter, and exhibit the same horrid grimaces he had shown them before, without vouchsafing a word in reply. Vathek, no longer able to brook such insolence, immediately kicked him from the steps, instantly descending repeated his blow, and persisted with such assiduity, as incited all who were present to follow his example. Every foot was aimed at the Indian, and no sooner had any one given him a kick than he felt himself constrained to reiterate the stroke.

The stranger afforded them no small entertainment; for being both short and plump, he collected himself into a ball and rolled round on all sides at the blows of his assailants, who pressed after him wherever he turned, with an eagerness beyond conception, whilst their numbers were every moment increasing. The ball, indeed, in passing from one apartment to another, drew every person after it that came in its way, insomuch that the whole palace was thrown into confusion, and resounded with a tremendous clamour. The women of the harem, amazed at the uproar, flew to their blinds to discover the cause, but no sooner did they catch a glimpse of the ball than feeling themselves unable to refrain, they broke from the clutches of their eunuchs, who to stop their flight pinched them till they bled,

[10] *The Prime Vizier.* Vazir, Vezir, or as we express it, Vizier, literally signifies a porter; and by metaphor, the minister who bears the principal burden of the state.

but in vain; whilst themselves, though trembling with terror at the escape of their charge, were as incapable of resisting the attraction.

The Indian, after having traversed the halls, galleries, chambers, kitchens, gardens, and stables of the palace, at last took his course through the courts, whilst the Caliph, pursuing him closer than the rest, bestowed as many kicks as he possibly could, yet not without receiving now and then one, which his competitors, in their eagerness, designed for the ball.

Carathis, Morakanabad, and two or three old viziers whose wisdom had hitherto withstood the attraction, wishing to prevent Vathek from exposing himself in the presence of his subjects, fell down in his way to impede the pursuit, but he, regardless of their obstruction, leaped over their heads, and went on as before. They then ordered the muezzins to call the people to prayers, both for the sake of getting them out of the way, and of endeavouring by their petitions to avert the calamity; but neither of these expedients was a whit more successful. The sight of this fatal ball was alone sufficient to draw after it every beholder. The muezzins themselves, though they saw it but at a distance, hastened down from their minarets and mixed with the crowd, which continued to increase in so surprising a manner, that scarce an inhabitant was left in Samarah, except the aged, the sick confined to their beds, and infants at the breast, whose nurses could run more nimbly without them. Even Carathis, Morakanabad, and the rest, were all become of the party.

The shrill screams of the females who had broken from their apartments, and were unable to extricate themselves from the pressure of the crowd, together with those of the eunuchs jostling after them, terrified lest their charge should escape from their sight, increased by the execrations of husbands urging forward and menacing both, kicks given and received, stumblings and overthrows at every step, in a word, the confusion that universally prevailed, rendered Samarah like a city taken by storm, and devoted to absolute plunder.

At last the cursed Indian, who still preserved his rotundity of figure, after passing through all the streets and public places, and leaving them empty, rolled onwards to the plain of Catoul, and traversed the valley at the foot of the mountain of the four fountains.

As a continual fall of water had excavated an immense gulph in the valley, whose opposite side was closed in by a steep acclivity, the Caliph and his attendants were apprehensive lest the ball should bound into the chasm, and to prevent it, redoubled their efforts, but in vain. The Indian persevered in his onward direction, and as had been apprehended, glancing from the precipice with the rapidity of lightning, was lost in the gulph below.

Vathek would have followed the perfidious Giaour, had not an invisible agency arrested his progress. The multitude that pressed after him were at once checked in the same manner, and a calm instantaneously ensued. They all gazed at each other with an air of astonishment; and notwithstanding that the loss of veils and turbans, together with torn habits, and dust blended with sweat, presented a most laughable spectacle, there was not one smile to be seen; on the contrary, all with looks of confusion and sadness returned in silence to Samarah, and retired to their inmost apartments, without ever reflecting that they had been impelled by an invisible power into the extravagance for which they reproached themselves: for it is but just, that men who so often arrogate to their own merit the good of which they are but instruments, should attribute to themselves the absurdities which they could not prevent.

The Caliph was the only person that refused to leave the valley. He commanded his tents to be pitched there, and stationed himself on the very edge of the precipice, in spite of the representations of Carathis and Morakanabad, who pointed out the hazard of its brink giving way, and the vicinity to the magician that had so severely tormented him. Vathek derided all their remonstrances; and having ordered a thousand flambeaus to be lighted, and directed his attendants to proceed in lighting more, lay down on the slippery margin, and attempted, by the help of this artificial splendour, to look through that gloom which all the fires of the empyrean had been insufficient to pervade. One while he fancied to himself voices arising from the depth of the gulph, at another he seemed to distinguish the accents of the Indian, but all was no more than the hollow murmur of waters, and the din of the cataracts that rushed from steep to steep, down the sides of the mountain.

Having passed the night in this cruel perturbation, the Caliph at day-break retired to his tent, where, without taking the least sustenance, he continued to doze till the dusk of evening began to come on; he then resumed his vigils as before, and persevered in observing them for many nights together. At length, fatigued with so successless an employment, he sought relief from change. To this end he sometimes paced with hasty strides across the plain; and as he wildly gazed at the stars, reproached them with having deceived him; but lo! on a sudden the clear blue sky appeared streaked over with streams of blood, which reached from the valley even to the city of Samarah. As this awful phenomenon seemed to touch his tower, Vathek at first thought of repairing thither to view it more distinctly, but feeling himself unable to advance, and being overcome with apprehension, he muffled up his face in his robe.

Terrifying as these prodigies were, this impression upon him was no more than momentary, and served only to stimulate his love of the marvellous. Instead, therefore, of returning to his palace, he persisted in the resolution of abiding where the Indian vanished from his view. One night, however, while he was walking as usual on the plain, the moon and the stars at once were eclipsed, and a total darkness ensued. The earth trembled beneath him, and a voice came forth, the voice of the Giaour, who in accents more sonorous than thunder, thus addressed him:

"Would'st thou devote thyself to me? adore then the terrestrial influences, and abjure Mahomet. On these conditions I will bring thee to the palace of subterranean fire: there shalt thou behold, in immense depositories, the treasures which the stars have promised thee, and which will be conferred by those intelligences whom thou shalt thus render propitious. It was from thence I brought my sabres; and it is there that Soliman Ben Daoud reposes, surrounded by the talismans that control the world."

The astonished Caliph trembled as he answered, yet in a style that showed him to be no novice in preternatural adventures:

"Where art thou? Be present to my eyes; dissipate the gloom that perplexes me, and of which I deem thee the cause. After the many flambeaus I have burnt to discover thee, thou mayest at least grant a glimpse of thy horrible visage."

"Abjure then Mahomet," replied the Indian, "and promise me full proofs of thy sincerity; otherwise thou shalt never behold me again."

The unhappy Caliph, instigated by insatiable curiosity, lavished his promises in the utmost profusion. The sky immediately brightened; and by the light of the planets, which seemed almost to blaze, Vathek beheld the earth open, and at the extremity of a vast black chasm a portal of ebony, before which stood the Indian, still blacker, holding in his hand a golden key, that caused the lock to resound.

"How," cried Vathek, "can I descend to thee, without the certainty of breaking my neck? Come take me, and instantly open the portal."

"Not so fast," replied the Indian, "impatient Caliph! Know that I am parched with thirst, and cannot open this door till my thirst be thoroughly appeased. I require the blood of fifty of the most beautiful sons of thy viziers and great men, or neither can my thirst nor thy curiosity be satisfied. Return to Samarah; procure for me this necessary libation; come back hither; throw it thyself into this chasm; and then shalt thou see!"

Having thus spoken, the Indian turned his back on the Caliph, who, incited by the suggestion of demons, resolved on the direful sacrifice. He now pretended to have regained his tranquillity, and set out for Samarah amidst the acclamations of a people who still loved him, and forbore not to rejoice when they believed him to have recovered his reason. So successfully did he conceal the emotion of his heart, that even Carathis and Morakanabad were equally deceived with the rest. Nothing was heard of but festivals and rejoicings. The ball, which no tongue had hitherto ventured to mention, was again brought on the tapis. A general laugh went round; though many, still smarting under the hands of the surgeon, from the hurts received in that memorable adventure, had no great reason for mirth.

The prevalence of this gay humour was not a little grateful to Vathek, as perceiving how much it conduced to his project. He put on the appearance of affability to every one; but especially to his viziers, and the grandees of his court, whom he failed not to regale with a sumptuous banquet, during which he insensibly inclined the conversation to the children of his guests. Having asked, with a good-natured air, who of them were blessed with the handsomest boys, every father at once asserted the pretensions of his own; and the contest imperceptibly grew so warm, that nothing could have with-holden them from coming to blows but their profound reverence for the person of the Caliph. Under the pretence, therefore, of reconciling the disputants, Vathek took upon him to decide; and with this view commanded the boys to be brought.

It was not long before a troop of these poor children made their appearance, all equipped by their fond mothers with such ornaments as might give the greatest relief to their beauty, or most advantageously display the graces of their age. But whilst this brilliant assemblage attracted the eyes and hearts of every one besides, the Caliph scrutinized each in his turn with a malignant avidity that passed for attention, and selected from their number the fifty whom he judged the Giaour would prefer.

With an equal show of kindness as before, he proposed to celebrate a festival on the plain, for the entertainment of his young favourites, who he said ought to rejoice still more than all at the restoration of his health, on account of the favours he intended for them.

The Caliph's proposal was received with the greatest delight, and soon published through Samarah. Litters, camels, and horses were prepared. Women and children, old men and young—every one placed himself in the station he chose. The cavalcade set forward, attended by all the confectioners in the city and its precincts. The populace, following on foot, composed an amazing crowd, and occasioned no little noise. All was joy; nor did any one call to mind what most of them had suffered when they first travelled the road they were now passing so gaily.

The evening was serene, the air refreshing, the sky clear, and the flowers exhaled their fragrance. The beams of the declining sun, whose mild splendour reposed on the summit of the mountain, shed a glow of ruddy light over its green declivity, and the white flocks sporting upon it. No sounds were audible, save the murmurs of the four fountains, and the reeds and voices of shepherds, calling to each other from different eminences.

The lovely innocents, proceeding to the destined sacrifice, added not a little to the hilarity of the scene. They approached the plain full of sportiveness; some coursing butterflies, others culling flowers, or picking up the shining little pebbles that attracted their notice. At intervals, they nimbly started from each other, for the sake of being caught again, and mutually imparting a thousand caresses.

The dreadful chasm, at whose bottom the portal of ebony was placed, began to appear at a distance. It looked like a black streak that divided the plain. Morakanabad and his companions took it for some work which the Caliph had ordered. Unhappy men! little did they surmise for what it was destined.

Vathek, not liking that they should examine it too nearly, stopped the procession, and ordered a spacious circle to be formed on this side, at some distance from the accursed chasm. The body-guard of eunuchs was detached, to measure out the lists intended for the games, and prepare ringles for the lines to keep off the crowd. The fifty competitors were soon stripped, and presented to the admiration of the spectators the suppleness and grace of their delicate limbs. Their eyes sparkled with a joy which those of their fond parents reflected. Every one offered wishes for the little candidate nearest his heart, and doubted not of his being victorious. A breathless suspense awaited the contest of these amiable and innocent victims.

The Caliph, availing himself of the first moment to retire from the crowd, advanced towards the chasm, and there heard, yet not without shuddering, the voice of the Indian; who, gnashing his teeth, eagerly demanded:

"Where are they? Where are they? perceivest thou not how my mouth waters?"

"Relentless Giaour!" answered Vathek, with emotion, "can nothing content thee but the massacre of these lovely victims? Ah! wert thou to behold their beauty, it must certainly move thy compassion."

"Perdition on thy compassion, babbler!" cried the Indian. "Give them me! instantly give them, or my portal shall be closed against thee for ever!"

"Not so loudly," replied the Caliph, blushing.

"I understand thee," returned the Giaour, with the grin of an ogre: "thou wantest to summon up more presence of mind. I will for a moment forbear."

During this exquisite dialogue the games went forward with all alacrity, and at length concluded, just as the twilight began to overcast the mountains. Vathek, who was still standing on the edge of the chasm, called out with all his might:

"Let my fifty little favourites approach me, separately; and let them come in the order of their success. To the first I will give my diamond bracelet; to the second my collar of emeralds; to the third my aigret of rubies; to the fourth my girdle of topazes; and to the rest, each a part of my dress, even down to my slippers."

This declaration was received with reiterated acclamations; and all extolled the liberality of a prince who would thus strip himself for the amusement of his subjects and the encouragement of the rising generation.

The Caliph in the mean while undressed himself by degrees; and raising his arm as high as he was able, made each of the prizes glitter in the air; but, whilst he delivered it with one hand to the child, who sprang forward to receive it, he with the other pushed the poor innocent into the gulph, where the Giaour, with a sullen muttering, incessantly repeated "More! more!"

This dreadful device was executed with so much dexterity, that the boy who was approaching him remained unconscious of the fate of his forerunner; and as to the spectators, the shades of evening, together with their distance, precluded them from perceiving any object distinctly. Vathek, having in this manner thrown in the last of the fifty, and expecting that the Giaour on receiving him would have presented the key, already fancied himself as great as Soliman, and consequently above being amenable for what he had done; when, to his utter amazement, the chasm closed, and the ground became as entire as the rest of the plain.

No language could express his rage and despair. He execrated the perfidy of the Indian; loaded him with the most infamous invectives; and stamped with his foot as resolving to be heard. He persisted in this demeanour till his strength failed him, and then fell on the earth like one void of sense. His viziers and grandees, who were nearer than the rest, supposed him at first to be sitting on the grass at play with their amiable children; but at length, prompted by doubt, they advanced towards the spot, and found the Caliph alone, who wildly demanded what they wanted.

"Our children! our children!" cried they.

"It is assuredly pleasant," said he, "to make me accountable for accidents. Your children, while at play, fell from the precipice that was here; and I should have experienced their fate had I not been saved by a sudden start back."

At these words, the fathers of the fifty boys cried out aloud: the mothers repeated their exclamations an octave higher; whilst the rest, without knowing the cause, soon drowned the voices of both, with still louder lamentations of their own.

"Our Caliph," said they, and the report soon circulated, "Our Caliph has played us this trick, to gratify his accursed Giaour. Let us punish him for his perfidy! let us avenge ourselves! let us avenge the blood of the innocent! let us throw this cruel Prince into the gulph that is near, and let his name be mentioned no more!"

At this rumour, and these menaces, Carathis, full of consternation, hastened to Morakanabad, and said:

"Vizier, you have lost two beautiful boys, and must necessarily be the most afflicted of fathers; but you are virtuous; save your master!"

"I will brave every hazard," replied the Vizier, "to rescue him from his present danger; but afterwards will abandon him to his fate. Bababalouk," continued he, "put yourself at the head of your Eunuchs, disperse the mob, and if possible bring back this unhappy Prince to his palace."

Bababalouk and his fraternity, felicitating each other in a low voice on their disability of ever being fathers, obeyed the mandate of the Vizier; who, seconding their exertions to the utmost of his power, at length accomplished his generous enterprise, and retired, as he resolved, to lament at his leisure.

No sooner had the Caliph re-entered his palace, than Carathis commanded the doors to be fastened; but perceiving the tumult to be still violent, and hearing the imprecations which resounded from all quarters, she said to her son:

"Whether the populace be right or wrong, it behoves you to provide for your safety: let us retire to your own apartment, and from thence, through the subterranean passage known only to ourselves, into your tower; there, with the assistance of the mutes who never leave it, we may be able to make some resistance. Bababalouk, supposing us to be still in the palace, will guard its avenues for his own sake; and we shall soon find, without the counsels of that blubberer Morakanabad, what expedient may be the best to adopt."

Vathek, without making the least reply, acquiesced in his mother's proposal, and repeated as he went:

"Nefarious Giaour! where art thou? hast thou not yet devoured those poor children? where are thy sabres? thy golden key? thy talismans?"

Carathis, who guessed from these interrogations a part of the truth, had no difficulty to apprehend in getting at the whole, as soon as he should be a little composed in his tower. This Princess was so far from being influenced by scruples that she was as wicked as woman could be, which is not saying a little, for the sex pique themselves on their superiority in every competition. The recital of the Caliph therefore occasioned neither terror nor surprise to his mother; she felt no emotion but from the promises of the Giaour; and said to her son:

"This Giaour, it must be confessed, is somewhat sanguinary in his taste, but the terrestrial powers are always terrible: nevertheless, what the one has promised and the others can confer, will prove a sufficient indemnification. No crimes should be thought too dear for such a reward. Forbear then to revile the Indian: you have not fulfilled the conditions to which his services are annexed. For instance, is not a sacrifice to the subterranean Genii required? and should we not be prepared to offer it as soon as the tumult is subsided? This charge I will take on myself, and have no doubt of succeeding by means of your treasures; which, as there are now so many others in store, may without fear be exhausted."

Accordingly, the Princess, who possessed the most consummate skill in the art of persuasion, went immediately back through the subterranean passage, and presenting herself to the populace from a window of the palace, began to harangue them with all the address of which she was mistress, whilst Bababalouk showered money from both hands amongst the crowd, who by these united means were soon appeased. Every person retired to his home, and Carathis returned to the tower.

Prayer at break of day was announced, when Carathis and Vathek ascended the steps which led to the summit of the tower, where they remained for some time, though the weather was lowering and wet. This impending gloom corresponded with their malignant dispositions; but when the sun began to break through the clouds, they ordered a pavilion to be raised as a screen from the intrusion of his beams. The Caliph, overcome with fatigue, sought refreshment from repose, at the same time hoping that significant dreams might attend on his slumbers; whilst the indefatigable Carathis, followed by a party of her mutes, descended to prepare whatever she judged proper for the oblation of the approaching night.

By secret stairs, known only to herself and her son, she first repaired to the mysterious recesses in which were deposited the mummies that had been brought from the catacombs of the ancient Pharaohs. Of these she ordered several to be taken. From thence she resorted to a gallery, where, under the guard of fifty female negroes, mute, and blind of the right eye, were preserved the oil of the most venomous serpents, rhinoceros' horns, and woods of a subtle and penetrating odour, procured from the interior of the Indies, together with a thousand other horrible rarieties. This collection had been formed for a purpose like the present, by Carathis herself, from a presentiment that she might one day enjoy some intercourse with the infernal powers, to whom she had ever been passionately attached, and to whose taste she was no stranger.

To familiarize herself the better with the horrors in view, the Princess remained in the company of her negresses, who squinted in the most amiable manner from the only eye they had, and leered with exquisite delight at the skulls and skeletons which Carathis had drawn forth from her cabinets, whose key she entrusted to no one; all of them making contortions, and uttering a frightful jargon, but very amusing to the Princess till at last, being stunned by their gibbering, and suffocated by the potency of their exhalations, she was forced to quit the gallery, after stripping it of a part of its treasures.

Whilst she was thus occupied, the Caliph, who instead of the visions he expected, had acquired in these insubstantial regions a voracious appetite, was greatly provoked at the negresses: for, having totally forgotten their deafness, he had impatiently asked them for food; and seeing them regardless of his demand, he began to cuff, pinch, and push them, till Carathis arrived to terminate a scene so indecent, to the great content of these miserable creatures, who having been brought up by her, understood all her signs, and communicated in the same way their thoughts in return.

"Son! what means all this?" said she, panting for breath. "I thought I heard as I came up, the shrieks of a thousand bats, tearing from their crannies in the recesses of a cavern, and it was the outcry only of these poor mutes, whom you were so unmercifully abusing. In truth you but ill deserve the admirable provision I have brought you."

"Give it me instantly!" exclaimed the Caliph: "I am perishing for hunger!"

"As to that," answered she, "you must have an excellent stomach if it can digest what I have been preparing."

"Be quick," replied the Caliph. "But oh, heavens! what horrors! What do you intend?"

"Come, come," returned Carathis, "be not so squeamish, but help me to arrange every thing properly, and you shall see that what you reject with such symptoms of disgust will soon complete your felicity. Let us get ready the pile for the sacrifice of to-night, and think not of eating till that is performed. Know you not that all solemn rites are preceded by a rigorous abstinence?"

The Caliph, not daring to object, abandoned himself to grief, and the wind that ravaged his entrails, whilst his mother went forward with the requisite operations. Phials of serpents' oil, mummies, and bones, were soon set in order on the balustrade of the tower. The pile began to rise; and in three hours was as many cubits high. At length, darkness approached, and Carathis having stripped herself to her inmost garment, clapped her hands in an impulse of ecstasy, and struck light with all her force. The mutes followed her example: but Vathek, extenuated with hunger and impatience, was unable to support himself, and fell down in a swoon. The sparks had already kindled the dry wood; the venomous oil burst into a thousand blue flames; the mummies, dissolving, emitted a thick dun vapour; and the rhinoceros' horns beginning to consume; all together diffused such a stench, that the Caliph, recovering, started from his trance and gazed wildly on the scene in full blaze around him. The oil gushed forth in a plentitude of streams; and the negresses, who supplied it without intermission, united their cries to those of the Princess. At last the fire became so violent, and the flames reflected from the polished marble so dazzling, that the Caliph, unable to withstand the heat and the blaze, effected his escape, and clambered up the imperial standard.

In the mean time, the inhabitants of Samarah, scared at the light which shone over the city, arose in haste, ascended their roofs, beheld the tower on fire, and hurried half-naked to the square. Their love to their sovereign immediately awoke; and apprehending him in danger of perishing in his tower, their whole thoughts were occupied with the means of his safety. Morakanabad flew from his retirement, wiped away his tears, and cried out for water like the rest. Bababalouk, whose olfactory nerves were more familiarized to magical odours, readily conjecturing that Carathis was engaged in her favourite amusements, strenuously exhorted them not to be alarmed. Him, however, they treated as an old poltroon; and forbore not to style him a rascally traitor. The camels and dromedaries were advancing with water, but no one knew by which way to enter the tower. Whilst the populace was obstinate in forcing the doors, a violent east wind drove such a volume of flame against them, as at first forced them off; but afterwards, rekindled their zeal. At the same time, the stench of the horns and mummies increasing, most of the crowd fell backward in a state of suffocation. Those that kept their feet mutually wondered at the cause of the smell, and admonished each other to retire. Morakanabad, more sick than the rest, remained in a piteous condition. Holding his nose with one hand, he persisted in his efforts with the other to burst open the doors, and obtain admission. A hundred and forty of the strongest and most resolute at length accomplished their purpose. Having gained the staircase by their violent exertions, they attained a great height in a quarter of an hour.

Carathis, alarmed at the signs of her mutes, advanced to the staircase, went down a few steps, and heard several voices calling out from below:

"You shall in a moment have water!"

Being rather alert, considering her age, she presently regained the top of the tower, and bade her son suspend the sacrifice for some minutes, adding:

"We shall soon be enabled to render it more grateful. Certain dolts of your subjects, imagining, no doubt, that we were on fire, have been rash enough to break through those doors, which had hitherto remained inviolate, for the sake of bringing up water. They are very kind, you must allow, so soon to forget the wrongs you have done them: but that is of little moment. Let us offer them to the Giaour. Let them come up: our mutes, who neither want strength nor experience, will soon despatch them, exhausted as they are with fatigue."

"Be it so," answered the Caliph, "provided we finish, and I dine."

In fact, these good people, out of breath from ascending eleven thousand stairs in such haste, and chagrined at having spilt, by the way, the water they had taken, were no sooner arrived at the top than the blaze of the flames and the fumes of the mummies at once overpowered their senses. It was a pity! for they beheld not the agreeable smile with which the mutes and the negresses adjusted the cord to their necks: these amiable personages rejoiced, however, no less at the scene. Never before had the ceremony of strangling been performed with so much facility. They all fell without the least resistance or struggle; so that Vathek, in the space of a few moments, found himself surrounded by the dead bodies of his most faithful subjects, all of which were thrown on the top of the pile.

Carathis, whose presence of mind never forsook her, perceiving that she had carcases sufficient to complete her oblation, commanded the chains to be stretched across the staircase, and the iron doors barricaded, that no more might come up.

No sooner were these orders obeyed, than the tower shook; the dead bodies vanished in the flames; which at once changed from a swarthy crimson to a bright rose colour. An ambient vapour emitted the most exquisite fragrance; the marble columns rang with harmonious sounds, and the liquefied horns diffused a delicious perfume. Carathis, in transports, anticipated the success of her enterprise; whilst the mutes and negresses, to whom these sweets had given the cholic, retired to their cells grumbling.

Scarcely were they gone, when, instead of the pile, horns, mummies, and ashes, the Caliph both saw and felt, with a degree of pleasure which he could not express, a table, covered with the most magnificent repast: flaggons of wine, and vases of exquisite sherbet, floating on snow. He availed himself, without scruple, of such an entertainment; and had already laid hands on a lamb stuffed with pistachios, whilst Carathis was privately drawing from a fillagreen urn, a parchment that seemed to be endless; and which had escaped the notice of her son. Totally occupied, in gratifying an importunate appetite, he left her to peruse it, without interruption; which having finished, she said to him, in an authoritative tone,

"Put an end to your gluttony, and hear the splendid promises with which you are favoured!" She then read, as follows:

"Vathek, my well-beloved, thou hast surpassed my hopes: my nostrils have been regaled by the savour of thy mummies, thy horns; and, still more, by the lives devoted on the pile. At the full of the moon, cause the bands of thy musicians, and thy tymbals, to be heard; depart from thy palace surrounded by all the pageants of majesty; thy most faithful slaves, thy best beloved wives; thy most magnificent litters; thy richest loaden camels; and set forward on thy way to Istakar. There await I thy coming. That is the region of wonders. There shalt thou receive the diadem of Gian Ben Gian,[11] the talismans of Soliman, and the treasures of the preadimite Sultans: there shalt thou be solaced with all kinds of delight. But, beware how thou enterest any dwelling on thy route, or thou shalt feel the effects of my anger."

The Caliph, who, notwithstanding his habitual luxury, had never before dined with so much satisfaction, gave full scope to the joy of these golden tidings, and betook himself to drinking anew. Carathis, whose antipathy to wine was by no means insuperable, failed not to supply a reason for every bumper, which they ironically quaffed to the health of Mahomet. This infernal liquor completed their impious temerity, and prompted them to utter a profusion of blasphemies. They gave a loose to their wit, at the expense of the ass of Balaam, the dog of the seven sleepers, and the other animals admitted into the paradise of Mahomet. In this sprightly humour they descended the eleven thousand stairs, diverting themselves as they went at the anxious faces they saw on the square, through the oilets of the

---

[11] *Gian Ben Gian.* By this appellation was distinguished the monarch of that species of beings, whom the Arabians denominate *Gian* or *Ginn*, that is, *Genii*; and the Tarik Thabari, *Peres, Feez,* or *Faeries.*

tower, and at length arrived at the royal apartments by the subterranean passage. Bababalouk was parading to and fro, and issuing his mandates with great pomp to the eunuchs, who were snuffing the lights and painting the eyes of the Circassians. No sooner did he catch sight of the Caliph and his mother than he exclaimed,

"Hah! you have then, I perceive, escaped from the flames; I was not, however, altogether out of doubt."

"Of what moment is it to us what you thought or think?" cried Carathis "go, speed, tell Morakanabad that we immediately want him; and take care how you stop by the way to make your insipid reflections."

Morakanabad delayed not to obey the summons, and was received by Vathek and his mother with great solemnity. They told him with an air of composure and commiseration that the fire at the top of the tower was extinguished, but that it had cost the lives of the brave people who sought to assist them.

"Still more misfortunes!" cried Morakanabad with a sigh. "Ah, commander of the faithful, our holy prophet is certainly irritated against us! it behoves you to appease him."

"We will appease him hereafter," replied the Caliph, with a smile that augured nothing of good. "You will have leisure sufficient for your supplications during my absence; for this country is the bane of my health. I am disgusted with the mountain of the Four Fountains, and am resolved to go and drink of the stream of Rocnabad.[12] I long to refresh myself in the delightful valleys which it waters. Do you, with the advice of my mother, govern my dominions; and take care to supply whatever her experiments may demand; for you well know that our tower abounds in materials for the advancement of science."

The tower but ill suited Morakanabad's taste. Immense treasures had been lavished upon it, and nothing had he ever seen carried thither but female negroes, mutes, and abominable drugs. Nor did he know well what to think of Carathis, who like a chamelion could assume all possible colours. Her cursed eloquence had often driven the poor Mussulman to his last shifts. He considered, however, that if she possessed but few good qualities, her son had still fewer, and that the alternative, on the whole, would be in her favour. Consoled, therefore, with this reflection, he went in good spirits to soothe the populace, and make the proper arrangements for his master's journey.

Vathek, to conciliate the spirits of the subterranean palace, resolved that his expedition should be uncommonly splendid. With this view he confiscated on all sides the property of his subjects, whilst his worthy mother stripped the seraglios she visited of the gems they contained. She collected all the sempstresses and embroiderers of Samarah, and other cities, to the distance of sixty leagues, to prepare pavilions, palanquins, sofas, canopies, and litters, for the train of the monarch. There was not left in Masulipatan a single piece of chintz; and so much muslin had been bought up to dress out Bababalouk and the other black eunuchs, that there <u>remained not an</u> ell in the whole Irak of Babylon.

[12] *Rocnabad.* The stream thus denominated flows near the city of Schiraz. Its waters are uncommonly pure and limpid, and their banks swarded with the finest verdure.

During these preparations, Carathis, who never lost sight of her great object, which was to obtain favour with the powers of darkness, made select parties of the fairest and most delicate ladies of the city; but in the midst of their gaiety she contrived to introduce serpents amongst them, and to break pots of scorpions under the table. They all bit to a wonder, and Carathis would have left them to bite, were it not that to fill up the time, she now and then amused herself in curing their wounds with an excellent anodyne of her own invention; for this good princess abhorred being indolent.

Vathek, who was not altogether so active as his mother, devoted his time to the sole gratification of his senses, in the palaces which were severally dedicated to them. He disgusted himself no more with the divan or the mosque. One half of Samarah followed his example, whilst the other lamented the progress of corruption.

In the midst of these transactions, the embassy returned which had been sent in pious times to Mecca. It consisted of the most reverend moullahs,[13] who had fulfilled their commission, and brought back one of those precious besoms which are used to sweep the sacred caaba; a present truly worthy of the greatest potentate on earth!

The Caliph happened at this instant to be engaged in an apartment by no means adapted to the reception of embassies, though adorned with a certain magnificence, not only to render it agreeable, but also because he resorted to it frequently, and staid a considerable time together. Whilst occupied in this retreat, he heard the voice of Bababalouk calling out from between the door and the tapestry that hung before it:

"Here are the excellent Mahomet Ebn Edris al Shafei, and the seraphic Al Mouhadethin, who have brought the besom from Mecca, and with tears of joy entreat they may present it to your majesty in person."

"Let them bring the besom hither, it may be of use," said Vathek, who was still employed, not having quite racked off his wine.

"How!" answered Bababalouk, half aloud and amazed.

"Obey," replied the Caliph, "for it is my sovereign will; go instantly! vanish! for here will I receive the good folk who have thus filled thee with joy."

The eunuch departed muttering, and bade the venerable train attend him. A sacred rapture was diffused amongst these reverend old men. Though fatigued with the length of their expedition, they followed Bababalouk with an alertness almost miraculous, and felt themselves highly flattered as they swept along the stately porticos, that the Caliph would not receive them like ambassadors in ordinary, in his hall of audience. Soon reaching the interior of the harem (where, through blinds of persian they perceived large soft eyes, dark and blue, that went and came like lightning) penetrated with respect and wonder, and full of their celestial mission, they advanced in procession towards the small corridors that appeared to terminate in nothing, but nevertheless led to the cell where the Caliph

---

[13] *Moullahs*. Those among the Mahometans who were bred to the law had this title; and from their order the judges of cities and provinces were taken.

expected their coming.

"What! is the commander of the faithful sick?" said Ebn Edris al Shafei, in a low voice to his companion.

"I rather think he is in his oratory," answered Al Mouhadethin.

Vathek, who heard the dialogue, cried out "What imports it you how I am employed? approach without delay."

They advanced, and Bababalouk almost sunk with confusion,[14] whilst the Caliph, without showing himself, put forth his hand from behind the tapestry that hung before the door, and demanded of them the besom.

Having prostrated themselves as well as the corridor would permit, and even in a tolerable semi-circle, the venerable Al Shafei, drawing forth the besom from the embroidered and perfumed scarfs in which it had been enveloped, and secured from the profane gaze of vulgar eyes, arose from his associates and advanced with an air of the most awful solemnity towards the supposed oratory; but with what astonishment! with what horror was he seized!

Vathek, bursting out into a villainous laugh, snatched the besom from his trembling hand, and fixing upon it some cobwebs that hung suspended from the ceiling, gravely brushed away till not a single one remained.

The old men, overpowered with amazement, were unable to lift their beards from the ground; for as Vathek had carelessly left the tapestry between them half drawn, they were witnesses to the whole transaction. Their tears gushed forth on the marble. Al Mouhadethin swooned through mortification and fatigue, whilst the Caliph, throwing himself backward on his seat, shouted and clapped his hands without mercy. At last, addressing himself to Bababalouk:

"My dear black," said he, "go, regale these pious poor souls with my good wine from Shiraz; and as they can boast of having seen more of my palace than any one besides, let them also visit my office courts, and lead them out by the back steps that go to my stables." Having said this, he threw the besom in their face, and went to enjoy the laugh with Carathis.

Bababalouk did all in his power to console the ambassadors, but the two most infirm expired on the spot; the rest were carried to their beds, from whence, being heart-broken with sorrow and shame, they never arose.

The succeeding night, Vathek, attended by his mother, ascended the tower to see if everything were ready for his journey, for he had great faith in the influence of the stars. The planets appeared in their most favourable aspects. The Caliph, to enjoy so flattering a sight, supped gaily on the roof, and fancied that he heard, during his repast, loud shouts of laughter resound through the sky, in a manner that inspired the fullest assurance.

---

[14] *Bababalouk almost sunk with confusion, whilst, etc.* The heinousness of Vathek's profanation can only be judged of by an orthodox Mussulman; or one who recollects the ablution and prayer indispensably required on the exoneration of nature. Sale's Prelim. Disc. p. 139. Al Koran, ch. 4. Habesci's State of the Ottoman Empire, p. 93.

All was in motion at the palace; lights were kept burning through the whole of the night; the sound of implements, and of artisans finishing their work; the voices of women and their guardians who sung at their embroidery; all conspired to interrupt the stillness of nature, and infinitely delight the heart of Vathek, who imagined himself going in triumph to sit upon the throne of Soliman.

The people were not less satisfied than himself; all assisted to accelerate the moment which should rescue them from the wayward caprices of so extravagant a master.

The day preceding the departure of this infatuated prince was employed by Carathis in repeating to him the decrees of the mysterious parchment, which she had thoroughly gotten by heart; and in recommending him not to enter the habitation of any one by the way; "for well thou knowest," added she, "how liquorish thy taste is after good dishes and young damsels; let me therefore enjoin thee to be content with thy old cooks, who are the best in the world; and not to forget that in thy ambulatory seraglio there are three dozen pretty faces, which Bababalouk hath not yet unveiled. I, myself, have a great desire to watch over thy conduct, and visit the subterranean palace, which no doubt contains whatever can interest persons like us. There is nothing so pleasing as retiring to caverns; my taste for dead bodies and everything like mummy is decided; and I am confident thou wilt see the most exquisite of their kind. Forget me not then, but the moment thou art in possession of the talismans which are to open to thee the mineral kingdoms, and the centre of the earth itself, fail not to dispatch some trusty genius to take me and my cabinet, for the oil of the serpents I have pinched to death will be a pretty present to the Giaour, who cannot but be charmed with such dainties."

Scarcely had Carathis ended this edifying discourse, when the sun, setting behind the mountain of the Four Fountains, gave place to the rising moon. This planet being that evening at full, appeared of unusual beauty and magnitude in the eyes of the women, the eunuchs, and the pages, who were all impatient to set forward. The city re-echoed with shouts of joy and flourishing of trumpets. Nothing was visible but plumes nodding on pavilions, and aigrets shining in the mild lustre of the moon. The spacious square resembled an immense parterre, variegated with the most stately tulips of the east.

Arrayed in the robes which were only worn at the most distinguished ceremonials, and supported by his vizier and Bababalouk, the Caliph descended the grand staircase of the tower in the sight of all his people. He could not forbear pausing at intervals to admire the superb appearance which everywhere courted his view, whilst the whole multitude, even to the camels with their sumptuous burdens, knelt down before him. For some time a general stillness prevailed, which nothing happened to disturb, but the shrill screams of some eunuchs in the rear. These vigilant guards having remarked certain cages of the ladies swagging somewhat awry, and discovered that a few adventurous gallants had contrived to get in, soon dislodged the enraptured culprits, and consigned them with good commendations, to the surgeons of the serail. The majesty of so magnificent a spectacle was not, however, violated by incidents like these. Vathek, meanwhile, saluted the moon with an idolatrous air, that neither pleased Morakanabad nor the doctors of the law, any more than the viziers and grandees of his court, who were all assembled to enjoy the last view of their sovereign.

At length the clarions and trumpets from the top of the tower announced the prelude of departure. Though the instruments were in unison with each other, yet a singular dissonance was blended with their sounds. This proceeded from Carathis, who was singing her direful orisons to the Giaour, whilst the negresses and mutes supplied thorough bass without articulating a word. The good Mussulmans fancied that they heard the sullen hum of those nocturnal insects which presage evil, and importuned Vathek to beware how he ventured his sacred person.

On a given signal the great standard of the Califat was displayed; twenty thousand lances shone around it; and the Caliph, treading royally on the cloth of gold which had been spread for his feet, ascended his litter amidst the general awe that possessed his subjects.

The expedition commenced with the utmost order, and so entire a silence, that even the locusts were heard from the thickets on the plain of Catoul. Gaiety and good humour prevailing, six good leagues were past before the dawn; and the morning star was still glittering in the firmament when the whole of this numerous train had halted on the banks of the Tigris, where they encamped to repose for the rest of the day.

The three days that followed were spent in the same manner, but on the fourth the heavens looked angry, lightnings broke forth in frequent flashes, re-echoing peals of thunder succeeded, and the trembling Circassians clung with all their might to their ugly guardians. The Caliph himself was greatly inclined to take shelter in the large town of Gulchissar, the governor of which came forth to meet him, and tendered every kind of refreshment the place could supply. But having examined his tablets, he suffered the rain to soak him almost to the bone, notwithstanding the importunity of his first favourites. Though he began to regret the palace of the senses, yet he lost not sight of his enterprise, and his sanguine expectations confirmed his resolution. His geographers were ordered to attend him, but the weather proved so terrible, that these poor people exhibited a lamentable appearance; and as no long journeys had been undertaken since the time of Haroun al Raschid, their maps of the different countries were in a still worse plight than themselves. Every one was ignorant which way to turn; for Vathek, though well versed in the course of the heavens, no longer knew his situation on earth. He thundered even louder than the elements, and muttered forth certain hints of the bowstring which were not very soothing to literary ears. Disgusted at the toilsome weariness of the way, he determined to cross over the craggy heights, and follow the guidance of a peasant, who undertook to bring him, in four days, to Rocnabad. Remonstrances were all to no purpose, his resolution was fixed, and an invasion commenced on the province of the goats, who sped away in large troops before them. It was curious to view on these half calcined rocks camels richly caparisoned, and pavilions of gold and silk waving on their summits, which till then had never been covered, but with sapless thistles and fern.

The females and eunuchs uttered shrill wailings at the sight of the precipices below them, and the dreary prospects that opened in the vast gorges of the mountains. Before they could reach the ascent of the steepest rock night overtook them, and a boisterous tempest arose, which having rent the awnings of the palanquins and cages, exposed to the raw gusts the poor ladies within, who had never before felt so piercing a cold. The dark clouds that overcast the face of the sky deepened the horrors of this disastrous night, insomuch that nothing could be heard distinctly but the mewling of pages, and lamentations of sultanas.

To increase the general misfortune, the frightful uproar of wild beasts resounded at a distance, and there were soon perceived in the forest they were skirting the glaring of eyes which could belong only to devils or tigers. The pioneers, who as well as they could, had marked out a track, and a part of the advanced guard were devoured before they had been in the least apprised of their danger. The confusion that prevailed was extreme. Wolves, tigers, and other carnivorous animals, invited by the howling of their companions, flocked together from every quarter. The crushing of bones was heard on all sides, and a fearful rush of wings over head, for now vultures also began to be of the party.

The terror at length reached the main body of the troops which surrounded the monarch and his harem, at the distance of two leagues from the scene. Vathek (voluptuously reposed in his capacious litter upon cushions of silk, with two little pages beside him, of complexions more fair than the enamel of Franguestan, who were occupied in keeping off flies) was soundly asleep, and contemplating in his dreams the treasures of Soliman. The shrieks, however, of his wives awoke him with a start, and instead of the Giaour with his key of gold, he beheld Bababalouk full of consternation.

"Sire," exclaimed this good servant of the most potent of monarchs, "misfortune has arrived at its height; wild beasts, who entertain no more reverence for your sacred person than for that of a dead ass, have beset your camels and their drivers: thirty of the richest laden are already become their prey, as well as all your confectioners, your cooks, and purveyors, and unless our holy prophet should protect us, we shall have all eaten our last meal."

At the mention of eating, the Caliph lost all patience. He began to bellow, and even beat himself, for there was no seeing in the dark. The rumour every instant increased, and Bababalouk finding no good could be done with his master stopped both his ears against the hurly-burly of the harem, and called out aloud:

"Come, ladies and brothers! all hands to work! strike light in a moment! never shall it be said that the commander of the faithful served to regale these infidel brutes."

Though there wanted not in this bevy of beauties a sufficient number of capricious and wayward, yet, on the present occasion they were all compliance. Fires were visible in a twinkling in all their cages. Ten thousand torches were lighted at once. The Caliph himself seized a large one of wax; every person followed his example; and by kindling ropes ends dipped in oil and fastened on poles, an amazing blaze was spread. The rocks were covered with the splendour of sunshine. The trails of sparks wafted by the wind, communicated to the dry fern, of which there was plenty. Serpents were observed to crawl forth from their retreats with amazement and hissings, whilst the horses snorted, stamped the ground, tossed their noses in the air, and plunged about without mercy.

One of the forests of cedar that bordered their way took fire, and the branches that overhung the path extending their flames to the muslins and chintzes which covered the cages of the ladies, obliged them to jump out at the peril of their necks. Vathek, who vented on the occasion a thousand blasphemies, was himself compelled to touch with his sacred feet the naked earth.

Never had such an incident happened before. Full of mortification, shame and despondence, and not knowing how to walk, the ladies fell into the dirt.

"Must I go on foot," said one.

"Must I wet my feet," cried another.

"Must I soil my dress," asked a third.

"Execrable Bababalouk," exclaimed all; "Outcast of hell! what hadst thou to do with torches? Better were it to be eaten by tigers than to fall into our present condition; we are for ever undone. Not a porter is there in the army, nor a currier of camels but hath seen some part of our bodies, and what is worse, our very faces!"

On saying this, the most bashful amongst them hid their foreheads on the ground, whilst such as had more boldness flew at Bababalouk, but he, well apprised of their humour, and not wanting in shrewdness, betook himself to his heels along with his comrades, all dropping their torches and striking their tymbals.

It was not less light than in the brightest of the dog-days, and the weather was hot in proportion; but how degrading was the spectacle, to behold the Caliph bespattered like an ordinary mortal! As the exercise of his faculties seemed to be suspended, one of his Ethiopian wives (for he delighted in variety) clasped him in her arms, threw him upon her shoulder like a sack of dates, and finding that the fire was hemming them in, set off with no small expedition, considering the weight of her burden. The other ladies who had just learned the use of their feet followed her; their guards galloped after; and the camel drivers brought up the rear as fast as their charge would permit.

They soon reached the spot where the wild beasts had commenced the carnage, and which they had too much spirit to leave, notwithstanding the approaching tumult, and the luxurious supper they had made. Bababalouk nevertheless seized on a few of the plumpest, which were unable to budge from the place, and began to flay them with admirable adroitness. The cavalcade being got so far from the conflagration as that the heat felt rather grateful than violent, it was immediately resolved on to halt. The tattered chintzes were picked up; the scraps left by the wolves and tigers interred; and vengeance was taken on some dozens of vultures that were too much glutted to rise on the wing. The camels which had been left unmolested to make sal-ammoniac being numbered, and the ladies once more inclosed in their cages, the imperial tent was pitched on the levellest ground they could find.

Vathek, reposing upon a matress of down, and tolerably recovered from the jolting of the Ethiopian, who, to his feelings seemed the roughest trotting jade he had hitherto mounted, called out for something to eat; but alas! those delicate cakes which had been baked in silver ovens for his royal mouth, those rich manchets, amber comfits, flaggons of Schiraz wine, porcelain vases of snow, and grapes from the banks of the Tigris, were all irremediably lost; and nothing had Bababalouk to present in their stead, but a roasted wolf, vultures à la daube, aromatic herbs of the most acrid poignancy, rotten truffles, boiled thistles, and such other wild plants as must ulcerate the throat and parch up the tongue. Nor was he better provided in the article of drink, for he could procure nothing to accompany these irritating viands but a few phials of abominable brandy, which had been secreted by the scullions in their slippers.

Vathek made wry faces at so savage a repast, and Bababalouk answered them with shrugs and contortions. The Caliph however ate with tolerable appetite, and fell into a nap that lasted six hours. The splendour of the sun, reflected from the white cliffs of the mountains in spite of the curtains that inclosed him, at length disturbed his repose. He awoke terrified, and stung to the quick by those wormwood-coloured flies which emit from their wings a suffocating stench. The miserable monarch was perplexed how to act, though his wits were not idle in seeking expedients, whilst Bababalouk lay snoring amidst a swarm of those insects, that busily thronged to pay court to his nose. The little pages, famished with hunger, had dropped their fans on the ground, and exerted their dying voices in bitter reproaches on the Caliph, who now for the first time heard the language of truth.

Thus stimulated, he renewed his imprecations against the Giaour, and bestowed upon Mahomet some soothing expressions.

"Where am I?" cried he; "What are these dreadful rocks; these valleys of darkness? Are we arrived at the horrible Kaf?[15] Is the Simurgh[16] coming to pluck out my eyes as a punishment for undertaking this impious enterprise?"

Having said this, he bellowed like a calf, and turned himself towards an outlet in the side of his pavilion. But alas! what objects occurred to his view! on one side a plain of black sand that appeared to be unbounded, and on the other perpendicular crags bristled over with those abominable thistles which had so severely lacerated his tongue. He fancied, however, that he perceived amongst the brambles and briars some gigantic flowers, but was mistaken, for these were only the dangling palampores and variegated tatters of his gay retinue. As there were several clefts

[15] *Horrible Kaf.* This mountain, which in reality is no other than Caucasus, was supposed to surround the earth, like a ring encompassing a finger. The sun was believed to rise from one of its eminences (as over Octa, by the Latin poets) and to set on the opposite; whence "from Kaf to Kaf," signified from one extremity of the earth to the other.

[16] *The Simurgh.* This is that wonderful bird of the East concerning which so many marvels are told. It was not only endowed with reason, but possessed also the knowledge of every language. This creature relates of itself, that it had seen the great revolution of seven thousand years, twelve times, commence and close; and, that in its duration, the world had been seven times void of inhabitants, and as often replenished. The Simurgh is represented as a great friend to the race of Adam, and not less inimical to the Dives.

in the rock from whence water seemed to have flowed, Vathek applied his ear with the hope of catching the sound of some latent runnel, but could only distinguish the low murmurs of his people, who were repining at their journey, and complaining for the want of water.

"To what purpose," asked they, "have we been brought hither? Hath our Caliph another tower to build? or have the relentless Afrits[17] whom Carathis so much loves, fixed in this place their abode?"

At the name of Carathis, Vathek recollected the tablets he had received from his mother, who assured him they were fraught with preternatural qualities, and advised him to consult them as emergencies might require. Whilst he was engaged in turning them over, he heard a shout of joy, and a loud clapping of hands. The curtains of his pavilion were soon drawn back, and he beheld Bababalouk, followed by a troop of his favourites, conducting two dwarfs, each a cubit high, who brought between them a large basket of melons, oranges, and pomegranites. They were singing in the sweetest tones the words that follow:

"We dwell on the top of these rocks, in a cabin of rushes and canes; the eagles envy us our nest; a small spring supplies us with abdest, and we daily repeat prayers which the prophet approves. We love you, O commander of the faithful! our master, the good emir Fakreddin, loves you also; he reveres in your person the vicegerent of Mahomet. Little as we are, in us he confides; he knows our hearts to be good, as our bodies are contemptible, and hath placed us here to aid those who are bewildered on these dreary mountains. Last night, whilst we were occupied within our cell in reading the holy koran, a sudden hurricane blew out our lights and rocked our habitation. For two whole hours a palpable darkness prevailed: but we heard sounds at a distance which we conjectured to proceed from the bells of a cafila, passing over the rocks. Our ears were soon filled with deplorable shrieks, frightful roarings, and the sound of tymbals. Chilled with terror, we concluded that the Deggial[18] with his exterminating angels had sent forth their plagues on the earth. In the midst of these melancholy reflections, we perceived flames of the deepest red glow in the horizon, and found ourselves in a few moments covered with flakes of fire. Amazed at so strange an appearance, we took up the volume dictated by the blessed intelligence, and kneeling by the light of the fire that surrounded us, we recited the verse which says: 'Put no trust in any thing but the mercy of heaven; there is no help save in the holy prophet; the mountain of Kaf itself may tremble; it is the power of Alla only that cannot be moved.' After having pronounced these words, we felt consolation, and our minds were hushed into a sacred repose. Silence ensued, and our ears clearly distinguished a voice in the air, saying: 'Servants of my faithful servant, go down to the happy valley of Fakreddin; tell him that an illustrious opportunity now offers to satiate the thirst of his hospitable heart. The commander of true believers is this day bewildered

---

[17] *Afrits.* These were a kind of Medusa, or Lamia, supposed to be the most terrible and cruel of all the orders of the Dives. Herbelot, p. 66.

[18] *Deggial.* This word signifies properly a liar and imposter, but is applied by Mahometan writers to their Antichrist. He is described as having but one eye and eyebrow, and on his forehead the radicals of *cafer*, or infidel, are said to be impressed.

amongst these mountains, and stands in need of thy aid.' We obeyed with joy the angelic mission, and our master, filled with pious zeal, hath culled with his own hands these melons, oranges, and pomegranites. He is following us with a hundred dromedaries laden with the purest waters of his fountains, and is coming to kiss the fringe of your consecrated robe, and implore you to enter his humble habitation, which, placed amidst these barren wilds, resembles an emerald set in lead."

The dwarfs having ended their address, remained still standing, and with hands crossed upon their bosoms, preserved a respectful silence.

Vathek, in the midst of this curious harangue seized the basket, and long before it was finished, the fruits had dissolved in his mouth. As he continued to eat, his piety increased, and in the same breath which recited his prayers, he called for the koran and sugar.

Such was the state of his mind when the tablets, which were thrown by at the approach of the dwarfs, again attracted his eye. He took them up, but was ready to drop on the ground when he beheld, in large red characters, these words inscribed by Carathis, which were indeed enough to make him tremble.

"Beware of thy old doctors, and their puny messengers of but one cubit high; distrust their pious frauds; and instead of eating their melons, impale on a spit the bearers of them. Shouldst thou be such a fool as to visit them, the portal of the subterranean palace will be shut in thy face, and with such force as shall shake thee asunder; thy body shall be spit upon, and bats will engender in thy belly."

"To what tends this ominous rhapsody?" cries the Caliph; "and must I then perish in these deserts with thirst, whilst I may refresh myself in the valley of melons and cucumbers? Accursed be the Giaour with his portal of ebony! he hath made me dance attendance too long already. Besides, who shall prescribe laws to me? I, forsooth, must not enter any one's habitation! Be it so, but what one can I enter that is not my own."

Bababalouk, who lost not a syllable of this soliloquy, applauded it with all his heart; and the ladies, for the first time, agreed with him in opinion. The dwarfs were entertained, caressed, and seated with great ceremony on little cushions of satin. The symmetry of their persons was the subject of criticism; not an inch of them was suffered to pass unexamined. Nick-nacks and dainties were offered in profusion, but all were declined with respectful gravity. They clambered up the sides of the Caliph's seat, and placing themselves each on one of his shoulders, began to whisper prayers in his ears. Their tongues quivered like the leaves of a poplar, and the patience of Vathek was almost exhausted, when the acclamations of the troops announced the approach of Fakreddin, who was come with a hundred old grey-beards, and as many korans and dromedaries. They instantly set about their ablutions, and began to repeat the Bismillah. Vathek, to get rid of these officious monitors, followed their example, for his hands were burning.

The good Emir, who was punctiliously religious, and likewise a great dealer in compliments, made an harangue five times more prolix and insipid than his harbingers had already delivered. The Caliph, unable any longer to refrain, exclaimed:

"For the love of Mahomet, my dear Fakreddin, have done! let us proceed to your valley, and enjoy the fruits that heaven hath vouchsafed you." The hint of proceeding put all into motion. The venerable attendants of the emir set forward somewhat slowly, but Vathek having ordered his little pages, in private, to goad on the dromedaries, loud fits of laughter broke forth from the cages, for the unwieldy curvetting of these poor beasts, and the ridiculous distress of their superannuated riders afforded the ladies no small entertainment.

They descended, however, unhurt into the valley, by the large steps which the emir had cut in the rock; and already the murmuring of streams and the rustling of leaves began to catch their attention. The cavalcade soon entered a path, which was skirted by flowering shrubs, and extended to a vast wood of palm-trees whose branches overspread a building of hewn stone. This edifice was crowned with nine domes, and adorned with as many portals of bronze, on which was engraven the following inscription:

"This is the asylum of pilgrims, the refuge of travellers, and the depository of secrets for all parts of the world."

Nine pages beautiful as the day, and clothed in robes of Egyptian linen, very long and very modest, were standing at each door. They received the whole retinue with an easy and inviting air. Four of the most amiable placed the Caliph on a magnificent taktrevan; four others, somewhat less graceful, took charge of Bababalouk, who capered for joy at the snug little cabin that fell to his share; the pages that remained, waited on the rest of the train.

When every thing masculine was gone out of sight, the gate of a large inclosure on the right turned on its harmonious hinges, and a young female of a slender form came forth. Her light brown hair floated in the hazy breeze of the twilight. A troop of young maidens, like the Pleiades, attended her on tip-toe. They hastened to the pavilions that contained the sultanas; and the young lady gracefully bending said to them:

"Charming princesses, every thing is ready; we have prepared beds for your repose, and strewed your apartments with jasmine; no insects will keep off slumber from visiting your eyelids; we will dispel them with a thousand plumes. Come then, amiable ladies! refresh your delicate feet and your ivory limbs in baths of rose water, and by the light of perfumed lamps your servants will amuse you with tales."

The sultanas accepted with pleasure these obliging offers, and followed the young lady to the emir's harem, where we must for a moment leave them and return to the Caliph.

Vathek found himself beneath a vast dome illuminated by a thousand lamps of rock crystal, as many vases of the same material filled with excellent sherbet sparkled on a large table, where a profusion of viands were spread. Amongst others were sweetbreads stewed in milk of almonds, saffron soups, and lamb à la crême, of all of which the Caliph was amazingly fond. He took of each as much as he was able; testified his sense of the emir's friendship by the gaiety of his heart; and made the dwarfs dance against their will; for these little devotees durst not refuse the commander of the faithful. At last he spread himself on the sofa and slept sounder than he had ever before.

Beneath this dome a general silence prevailed, for there was nothing to disturb it but the jaws of Bababalouk, who had untrussed himself to eat with greater advantage, being anxious to make amends for his fast in the mountains. As his spirits were too high to admit of his sleeping, and not loving to be idle, he proposed with himself to visit the harem, and repair to his charge of the ladies, to examine if they had been properly lubricated with the balm of Mecca, if their eye-brows and tresses were in order, and in a word, to perform all the little offices they might need. He sought for a long time together, but without being able to find out the door. He durst not speak aloud for fear of disturbing the Caliph, and not a soul was stirring in the precincts of the palace. He almost despaired of effecting his purpose, when a low whispering just reached his ear: it came from the dwarfs, who were returned to their old occupation, and for the nine hundred and ninety-ninth time in their lives were reading over the koran. They very politely invited Bababalouk to be of their party, but his head was full of other concerns. The dwarfs, though scandalized at his dissolute morals, directed him to the apartments he wanted to find. His way thither lay through a hundred dark corridors, along which he groped as he went, and at last began to catch, from the extremity of a passage, the charming gossiping of women, which not a little delighted his heart.

"Ah, ah! what not yet asleep?" cried he, and taking long strides as he spoke, "did you not suspect me of abjuring my charge? I stayed but to finish what my master had left."

Two of the black eunuchs on hearing a voice so loud detached a party in haste, sabre in hand, to discover the cause, but presently was repeated on all sides:

"'Tis only Bababalouk, no one but Bababalouk!"

This circumspect guardian having gone up to a thin veil of carnation colour silk that hung before the doorway, distinguished by means of a softened splendour that shone through it, an oval bath of dark porphyry surrounded by curtains festooned in large folds. Through the apertures between them, as they were not drawn close, groups of young slaves were visible, amongst whom Bababalouk perceived his pupils indulgingly expanding their arms, as if to embrace the perfumed water, and refresh themselves after their fatigues. The looks of tender languor, their confidential whispers, and the enchanting smiles with which they were imparted, the exquisite fragrance of the roses, all combined to inspire a voluptuousness which even Bababalouk himself was scarce able to withstand.

He summoned up, however, his usual solemnity, and in the peremptory tone of authority commanded the ladies instantly to leave the bath. Whilst he was issuing these mandates, the young Nouronihar, daughter of the emir, who was sprightly as an antelope, and full of wanton gaiety, beckoned one of her slaves to let down the great swing, which was suspended to the ceiling by cords of silk, and whilst this was doing winked to her companions in the bath, who chagrined to be forced from so soothing a state of indolence, began to twist it round Bababalouk, and teaze him with a thousand vagaries.

When Nouronihar perceived that he was exhausted with fatigue, she accosted him with an arch air of respectful concern, and said:

"My lord, it is not by any means decent that the chief eunuch of the Caliph our sovereign should thus continue standing, deign but to recline your graceful person upon this sofa, which will burst with vexation if it have not the honour to receive you."

Caught by these flattering accents, Bababalouk gallantly replied:

"Delight of the apple of my eye! I accept the invitation of thy honied lips, and to say truth, my senses are dazzled with the radiance that beams from thy charms."

"Repose, then, at your ease," replied the beauty, and placed him on the pretended sofa, which, quicker than lightning, gave way all at once. The rest of the women having aptly conceived her design, sprang naked from the bath and plied the swing with such unmerciful jerks, that it swept through the whole compass of a very lofty dome, and took from the poor victim all power of respiration. Sometimes his feet rased the surface of the water, and at others the skylight almost flattened his nose. In vain did he pierce the air with the cries of a voice that resembled the ringing of a cracked basin, for their peals of laughter were still more predominant.

Nouronihar in the inebriety of youthful spirits being used only to eunuchs of ordinary harems, and having never seen any thing so royal and disgusting, was far more diverted than all of the rest. She began to parody some Persian verses, and sung with an accent most demurely piquant:

> "O gentle white dove as thou soar'st through the air,
> Vouchsafe one kind glance on the mate of thy love:
> Melodious Philomel I am thy rose;
> Warble some couplet to ravish my heart!"

The sultanas and their slaves stimulated by these pleasantries persevered at the swing with such unremitted assiduity, that at length the cord which had secured it snapped suddenly asunder, and Bababalouk fell floundering like a turtle to the bottom of the bath. This accident occasioned a universal shout. Twelve little doors till now unobserved flew open at once, and the ladies in an instant made their escape, after throwing all the towels on his head, and putting out the lights that remained.

The deplorable animal, in water to the chin, overwhelmed with darkness, and unable to extricate himself from the warp that embarrassed him, was still doomed to hear for his further consolation, the fresh bursts of merriment his disaster occasioned. He bustled but in vain to get from the bath, for the margin was become so slippery with the oil spilt in breaking the lamps, that at every effort he slid back with a plunge, which resounded aloud through the hollow of the dome. These cursed peals of laughter at every relapse were redoubled, and he, who thought the place infested rather by devils than women, resolved to cease groping, and abide in the bath, where he amused himself with soliloquies interspersed with imprecations, of which his malicious neighbours, reclining on down, suffered not an accent to escape. In this delectable plight the morning surprised him. The Caliph, wondering at his absence, had caused him to be everywhere sought for. At last he was drawn forth almost smothered from the whisp of linen, and wet even to the marrow. Limping, and chattering his teeth, he appeared before his master, who inquired what was the matter, and how he came soused in so strange a pickle.

"And why did you enter this cursed lodge?" answered Bababalouk, gruffly. "Ought a monarch like you to visit with his harem the abode of a grey bearded emir who knows nothing of life? And with what gracious damsels does the place too abound! Fancy to yourself how they have soaked me like a burnt crust, and made me dance like a jack-pudding the live-long night through on their damnable swing. What an excellent lesson for your sultanas to follow, into whom I have instilled such reserve and decorum!"

Vathek, comprehending not a syllable of all this invective, obliged him to relate minutely the transaction; but instead of sympathising with the miserable sufferer, he laughed immoderately at the device of the swing, and the figure of Bababalouk mounting upon it. The stung eunuch could scarcely preserve the semblance of respect.

"Aye, laugh my lord! laugh," said he, "but I wish this Nouronihar would play some trick on you; she is too wicked to spare even majesty itself."

These words made for the present but a slight impression on the Caliph, but they not long after recurred to his mind.

This conversation was cut short by Fakreddin, who came to request that Vathek would join in the prayers and ablutions to be solemnized on a spacious meadow, watered by innumerable streams. The Caliph found the waters refreshing, but the prayers abominably irksome. He diverted himself however with the multitude of Calenders,[19] Santons,[20] and Dervises[21] who were continually coming and going, but especially with the Brahmins,[22] Faquirs,[23] and other enthusiasts, who had travelled from the heart of India, and halted on their way with the emir. These latter had each of them some mummery peculiar to himself. One dragged a huge

---

[19] *Calenders.* These were a sort of men amongst the Mahometans who abandoned father and mother, wife and children, relations and possessions, to wander through the world, under a pretence of religion, entirely subsisting on the fortuitous bounty of those they had the address to dupe. Herbelot, Suppl. p. 204.

[20] *Santons.* A body of religionists who were also called *Abdals*, and pretended to be inspired with the most enthusiastic raptures of divine love. They were regarded by the vulgar as saints. Olearius, Tom. I. p. 971. Herbelot, p. 5.

[21] *Dervises.* The term *dervise* signifies a poor man, and is the general appellation by which a religious sect amongst the Mahometans is named.

[22] *Brahmins.* These constituted the principal caste of the Indians, according to whose doctrines Brahma, from whom they are called, is the first of the three created beings by whom the world was made. This Brahma is said to have communicated to the Indians four books, in which all the sciences and ceremonies of their religion are comprised.

[23] *Faquirs.* This sect were a kind of religious anchorites, who spent their whole lives in the severest austerities and mortification.

chain where ever he went, another an ourang-outang, whilst a third was furnished with scourges, and all performed to a charm. Some clambered up trees, holding one foot in the air; others poised themselves over a fire, and without mercy fillipped their noses. There were some amongst them that cherished vermin, which were not ungrateful in requiting their caresses. These rambling fanatics revolted the hearts of the Dervises, the Calenders, and Santons; however the vehemence of their aversion soon subsided under the hope that the presence of the Caliph would cure their folly, and convert them to the Mussulman faith. But alas! how great was their disappointment! for Vathek, instead of preaching to them, treated them as buffoons; bade them present his compliments to Visnow and Ixhora, and discovered a predilection for a squat old man from the Isle of Serendib, who was more ridiculous than any of the rest.

"Come," said he, "for the love of your gods, bestow a few slaps on your chops to amuse me."

The old fellow offended at such an address began loudly to weep; but as he betrayed a villainous drivelling in his tears, the Caliph turned his back and listened to Bababalouk, who whispered, whilst he held the umbrella over him:

"Your majesty should be cautious of this odd assembly, which hath been collected I know not for what. Is it necessary to exhibit such spectacles to a mighty potentate, with interludes of talapoins more mangy than dogs? Were I you, I would command a fire to be kindled, and at once purge the earth of the emir, his harem, and all his menagery."

"Tush, dolt," answered Vathek, "and know that all this infinitely charms me. Nor shall I leave the meadow till I have visited every hive of these pious mendicants."

Where ever the Caliph directed his course, objects of pity were sure to swarm round him: the blind, the purblind, smarts without noses, damsels without ears, each to extol the munificence of Fakreddin, who, as well as his attendant greybeards, dealt about gratis plasters and cataplasms to all that applied. At noon a superb corps of cripples made its appearance; and soon after advanced by platoons on the plain the completest association of invalids that had ever been embodied till then. The blind went groping with the blind; the lame limped on together; and the maimed made gestures to each other with the only arm that remained. The sides of a considerable waterfall were crowded by the deaf, amongst whom were some from Pegu, with ears uncommonly handsome and large, but were still less able to hear than the rest. Nor were there wanting others in abundance with hump backs, wenny necks, and even horns of an exquisite polish.

The emir, to aggrandize the solemnity of the festival in honour of his illustrious visitant, ordered the turf to be spread on all sides with skins and table cloths, upon which were served up for the good mussulmans pilaus of every hue, with other orthodox dishes, and by the express order of Vathek, who was shamefully tolerant, small plates of abominations for regaling the rest. This prince on seeing so many mouths put in motion began to think it time for employing his own. In spite, therefore, of every remonstrance from the chief of his eunuchs, he resolved to have a dinner dressed on the spot. The complaisant emir immediately gave orders for a table to be placed in the shade of the willows. The first service consisted of fish, which they drew from a river flowing over sands of gold, at the foot of a lofty hill: these were broiled as fast as taken, and served up with a sauce of vinegar and small herbs that grew on Mount Sinai; for everything with the emir was excellent and pious.

The dessert was not quite set on when the sound of lutes from the hill was repeated by the echoes of the neighbouring mountains. The Caliph with an emotion of pleasure and surprise, had no sooner raised up his head than a handful of jasmine dropped on his face. An abundance of tittering succeeded this frolic, and instantly appeared through the bushes the elegant forms of several young females, skipping and bounding like roes. The fragrance diffused from their hair struck the sense of Vathek, who in an ecstasy, suspending his repast, said to Bababalouk:

"Are the Peries[24] come down from their spheres? Note her in particular whose form is so perfect, venturously running on the brink of the precipice, and turning back her head as regardless of nothing but the graceful flow of her robe. With what captivating impatience doth she contend with the bushes for her veil? Could it be she who threw the jasmine at me?"

"Aye, she it was; and you too would she throw from the top of the rock," answered Bababalouk, "for that is my good friend Nouronihar, who so kindly lent me her swing. My dear lord and master," added he, twisting a twig that hung by the rind from a willow, "let me correct her for her want of respect: the emir will have no reason to complain, since (bating what I owe to his piety) he is much to be censured for keeping a troop of girls on the mountains, whose sharp air gives their blood too brisk a circulation."

"Peace, blasphemer!" said the Caliph: "speak not thus of her who over her mountains leads my heart a willing captive. Contrive, rather, that my eyes may be fixed upon hers—that I may respire her sweet breath, as she bounds panting along these delightful wilds!"

On saying these words, Vathek extended his arms towards the hill, and directing his eyes with an anxiety unknown to him before, endeavoured to keep within view the object that enthralled his soul; but her course was as difficult to follow as the flight of one of those beautiful blue butterflies of Cachmere, which are at once so volatile and rare.

The Caliph, not satisfied with seeing, wished also to hear Nouronihar, and eagerly turned to catch the sound of her voice. At last he distinguished her whispering to one of her companions behind the thicket from whence she had thrown the jasmine:

"A Caliph, it must be owned, is a fine thing to see, but my little Gulchenrouz is much more amiable; one lock of his hair is of more value to me than the richest embroidery of the Indies. I had rather that his teeth should mischievously press my finger, than the richest ring of the imperial treasure. Where have you left him,

[24] *Peries.* The word Peri, in the Persian language, signifies that beautiful race of creatures which constitutes the link between angels and men.

Sutlememe? and why is he now not here?"

The agitated Caliph still wished to hear more, but she immediately retired with all her attendants. The fond monarch pursued her with his eyes till she was gone out of sight, and then continued like a bewildered and benighted traveller, from whom the clouds had obscured the constellation that guided his way. The curtain of night seemed dropped before him—everything appeared discoloured. The falling waters filled his soul with dejection, and his tears trickled down the jasamines he had caught from Nouronihar, and placed in his inflamed bosom. He snatched up a shining pebble to remind him of the scene where he felt the first tumults of love. Two hours were elapsed, and evening drew on before he could resolve to depart from the place. He often, but in vain, attempted to go: a soft languor enervated the powers of his mind. Extending himself on the brink of the stream, he turned his eyes towards the blue summits of the mountain, and exclaimed:

"What concealest thou behind thee? what is passing in thy solitudes? Whither is she gone? O heaven! perhaps she is now wandering in the grottoes with her happy Gulchenrouz!"

In the mean time the damps began to descend, and the emir, solicitous for the health of the Caliph, ordered the imperial litter to be brought. Vathek, absorbed in his reveries, was imperceptibly removed and conveyed back to the saloon that received him the evening before.

But let us leave the Caliph immersed in his new passion, and attend Nouronihar beyond the rocks, where she had again joined her beloved Gulchenrouz. This Gulchenrouz was the son of Ali Hassan, brother to the emir, and the most delicate and lovely creature in the world. Ali Hassan, who had been absent ten years on a voyage to the unknown seas, committed at his departure this child, the only survivor of many, to the care and protection of his brother. Gulchenrouz could write in various characters with precision, and paint upon vellum the most elegant arabesques that fancy could devise. His sweet voice accompanied the lute in the most enchanting manner; and when he sung the loves of Megnoun and Leileh, or some unfortunate lovers of ancient days, tears insensibly overflowed the cheeks of his auditors. The verses he composed (for like Megnoun, he too was a poet) inspired that unresisting languor so frequently fatal to the female heart. The women all doated upon him, for though he had passed his thirteenth year, they still detained him in the harem. His dancing was light as the gossamer waved by the zephyrs of spring; but his arms which twined so gracefully with those of the young girls in the dance, could neither dart the lance in the chase, nor curb the steeds that pastured his uncle's domains. The bow, however, he drew with a certain aim, and would have excelled his competitors in the race, could he have broken the ties that bound him to Nouronihar.

The two brothers had mutually engaged their children to each other; and Nouronihar loved her cousin more than her eyes. Both had the same tastes and amusements; the same long languishing looks; the same tresses; the same fair complexions; and when Gulchenrouz appeared in the dress of his cousin, he seemed to be more feminine than even herself. If at any time he left the harem to visit Fakreddin, it was with all the bashfulness of a fawn that consciously ventures from the lair of its dam; he was however wanton enough to mock the solemn old grey-beards to whom he was subject, though sure to be rated without mercy in return. Whenever this happened, he would plunge into the recesses of the harem, and sobbing take refuge in the arms of Nouronihar, who loved even his faults beyond the virtues of others.

It fell out this evening that after leaving the Caliph in the meadow, she ran with Gulchenrouz over the green sward of the mountain that sheltered the vale, where Fakreddin had chosen to reside. The sun was dilated on the edge of the horizon; and the young people, whose fancies were lively and inventive, imagined they beheld in the gorgeous clouds of the west the domes of Shadukiam and Ambreabad, where the Peries have fixed their abode. Nouronihar, sitting on the slope of the hill, supported on her knees the perfumed head of Gulchenrouz. The air was calm, and no sound stirred but the voices of other young girls who were drawing cool water from the streams below. The unexpected arrival of the Caliph, and the splendour that marked his appearance, had already filled with emotion the ardent soul of Nouronihar. Her vanity irresistibly prompted her to pique the prince's attention, and this she before took good care to effect whilst he picked up the jasamine she had thrown upon him. But when Gulchenrouz asked after the flowers he had culled for her bosom, Nouronihar was all in confusion. She hastily kissed his forehead, arose in a flutter, and walked with unequal steps on the border of the precipice. Night advanced, and the pure gold of the setting sun had yielded to a sanguine red, the glow of which, like the reflection of a burning furnace, flushed Nouronihar's animated countenance. Gulchenrouz alarmed at the agitation of his cousin, said to her with a supplicating accent:

"Let us be gone; the sky looks portentious: the tamarisks tremble more than common; and the raw wind chills my very heart. Come, let us be gone, 'tis a melancholy night."

Then taking hold of her hand he drew it towards the path he besought her to go. Nouronihar unconsciously followed the attraction, for a thousand strange imaginations occupied her spirit. She passed the large round of honeysuckles, her favourite resort, without ever vouchsafing it a glance, yet Gulchenrouz could not help snatching off a few shoots in his way, though he ran as if a wild beast were behind.

The young females seeing him approach in such haste, and according to custom expecting a dance, instantly assembled in a circle and took each other by the hand, but Gulchenrouz coming up out of breath, fell down at once on the grass. This accident struck with consternation the whole of this frolicsome party, whilst Nouronihar, half distracted, and overcome both by the violence of her exercise and the tumult of her thoughts, sunk feebly down at his side, cherished his cold hands in her bosom, and chafed his temples with a fragrant unguent. At length he came to himself, and wrapping up his head in the robe of his cousin, entreated that she would not return to the harem. He was afraid of being snapped at by Shaban his tutor, a wrinkled old eunuch of a surly disposition, for having interrupted the stated walk of Nouronihar, he dreaded lest the churl should take it amiss. The whole of this sprightly group, sitting round upon a mossy knole, began to entertain themselves with various pastimes, whilst their superintendents the eunuchs were gravely conversing at a distance. The nurse of the emir's daughter observing her pupil sit ruminating with her eyes on the ground, endeavoured to amuse her with diverting tales, to which Gulchenrouz, who had already forgotten his inquietudes, listened with a breathless attention. He laughed; he clapped his hands; and passed a hundred little tricks on the whole of the company, without omitting the eunuchs, whom he provoked to run after him, in spite of their age and decrepitude.

During these occurrences the moon arose, the wind subsided, and the evening became so serene and inviting that a resolution was taken to sup on the spot. Sutlememe, who excelled in dressing a salad, having filled large bowls of porcelain with eggs of small birds, curds turned with citron juice, slices of cucumber, and the inmost leaves of delicate herbs, handed it round from one to another, and gave each their shares in a large spoon of cocknos. Gulchenrouz nestling as usual in the bosom of Nouronihar, pouted out his vermillion little lips against the offer of Sutlememe, and would take it only from the hand of his cousin, on whose mouth he hung like a bee inebriated with the quintessence of flowers. One of the eunuchs ran to fetch melons, whilst others were employed in showering down almonds from the branches that overhung this amiable party.

In the midst of this festive scene there appeared a light on the top of the highest mountain, which attracted the notice of every eye. This light was not less bright than the moon when at full, and might have been taken for her had it not been that the moon was already risen. The phenomenon occasioned a general surprise, and no one could conjecture the cause. It could not be a fire, for the light was clear and bluish; nor had meteors ever been seen of that magnitude or splendour. This strange light faded for a moment, and immediately renewed its brightness. It first appeared motionless at the foot of the rock, whence it darted in an instant to sparkle in a thicket of palm trees, from thence it glided along the torrent, and at last fixed in a glen that was narrow and dark. The moment it had taken its direction, Gulchenrouz, whose heart always trembled at any thing sudden or rare, drew Nouronihar by the robe, and anxiously requested her to return to the harem. The women were importunate in seconding the entreaty, but the curiosity of the emir's daughter prevailed. She not only refused to go back, but resolved at all hazards to pursue the appearance. Whilst they were debating what was best to be done, the light shot forth so dazzling a blaze that they all fled away shrieking. Nouronihar followed them a few steps, but coming to the turn of a little bye path stopped, and went back alone. As she ran with an alertness peculiar to herself, it was not long before she came to the place where they had just been supping. The globe of fire now appeared stationary in the glen, and burned in majestic stillness. Nouronihar compressing her hands upon her bosom, hesitated for some moments to advance. The solitude of her situation was new; the silence of the night awful; and every object inspired sensations which till then she never had felt. The affright of Gulchenrouz recurred to her mind; and she a thousand times turned to go back, but this luminous appearance was always before her. Urged on by an irresistible impulse, she continued to approach it in defiance of every obstacle that opposed her progress.

At length she arrived at the opening of the glen, but instead of coming up to the light, she found herself surrounded by darkness, except that at a considerable distance a faint spark glimmered by fits. She stopped a second time: the sound of waterfalls mingling their murmurs, the hollow rustlings amongst the palm branches, and the funereal screams of the birds from their rifted trunks, all conspired to fill her with terror. She imagined every moment that she trod on some venomous reptile. All the stories of malignant Dives, and dismal Goules thronged into her memory, but her curiosity was notwithstanding more predominant than her fears. She therefore firmly entered a winding track that led towards the spark, but being a stranger to the path, she had not gone far till she began to repent of her rashness.

"Alas!" said she, "that I were but in those secure and illuminated apartments where my evenings glided on with Gulchenrouz! Dear child, how would thy heart flutter with terror wert thou wandering in these wild solitudes like me."

At the close of this apostrophe she regained her road, and coming to steps hewn out in the rock ascended them undismayed. The light, which was now gradually enlarging, appeared above her on the summit of the mountain. At length she distinguished a plaintive and melodious union of voices proceeding from a sort of cavern, that resembled the dirges which are sung over tombs. A sound likewise like that which arises from the filling of baths, at the same time struck her ear. She continued ascending, and discovered large wax torches in full blaze planted here and there in the fissures of the rock. This preparation filled her with fear, whilst the subtle and potent odour which the torches exhaled caused her to sink almost lifeless at the entrance of the grot.

Casting her eyes within in this kind of trance, she beheld a large cistern of gold filled with a water, whose vapour distilled on her face a dew of the essence of roses. A soft symphony resounded through the grot. On the sides of the cistern she noticed appendages of royalty; diadems and feathers of the heron, all sparkling with carbuncles. Whilst her attention was fixed on this display of magnificence, the music ceased, and a voice instantly demanded:

"For what monarch were these torches kindled, this bath prepared, and these habiliments? which belong not only to the sovereigns of the earth, but even to the talismanic powers!"

To which a second voice answered:

"They are for the charming daughter of the emir Fakreddin."

"What," replied the first, "for that trifler who consumes her time with a giddy child, immersed in softness, and who at best can make but an enervated husband?"

"And can she," rejoined the other voice, "be amused with such empty trifles, whilst the Caliph, the sovereign of the world, he who is destined to enjoy the treasures of the preadimite sultans, a prince six feet high, and whose eyes pervade the inmost soul of a female, is inflamed with the love of her? no, she will be wise enough to answer that passion alone that can aggrandize her glory. No doubt she will, and despise the puppet of her fancy; then all the riches this place contains, as well as the carbuncle of Giamschid shall be hers."

"You judge right," returned the first voice, "and I haste to Istakar to prepare the palace of subterranean fire for the reception of the bridal pair."

The voices ceased, the torches were extinguished, the most entire darkness succeeded, and Nouronihar recovering with a start, found herself reclined on a sofa in the harem of her father. She clapped her hands, and immediately came together Gulchenrouz and her women, who, in despair at having lost her, had despatched eunuchs to seek her in every direction. Shaban appeared with the rest, and began to reprimand her with an air of consequence:

"Little impertinent," said he, "whence got you false keys? or are you beloved of some genius that hath given you a picklock? I will try the extent of your power; come, to your chamber! through the two sky-lights, and expect not the company of Gulchenrouz. Be expeditious! I will shut you up in the double tower."

At these menaces Nouronihar indignantly raised her head, opened on Shaban her black eyes, which since the important dialogue of the enchanted grot were considerably enlarged, and said:

"Go, speak thus to slaves! but learn to reverence her who is born to give laws, and subject all to her power."

She was proceeding in the same style, but was interrupted by a sudden exclamation of,

"The Caliph! the Caliph!"

The curtains at once were thrown open, and the slaves prostrate in double rows, whilst poor little Gulchenrouz hid himself beneath the elevation of a sofa. At first appeared a file of black eunuchs trailing after them long trains of muslin embroidered with gold, and holding in their hands censers, which dispensed as they passed the grateful perfume of the wood of aloes. Next marched Bababalouk with a solemn strut, and tossing his head as not over pleased at the visit. Vathek came close after superbly robed; his gait was unembarrassed and noble, and his presence would have engaged admiration, though he had not been the sovereign of the world. He approached Nouronihar with a throbbing heart, and seemed enraptured at the full effulgence of her radiant eyes, of which he had before caught but a few glimpses; but she instantly depressed them, and her confusion augmented her beauty.

Bababalouk, who was a thorough adept in coincidences of this nature, and knew that the worst game should be played with the best face, immediately made a signal for all to retire, and no sooner did he perceive beneath the sofa the little one's feet, than he drew him forth without ceremony, set him upon his shoulders, and lavished on him as he went off a thousand odious caresses. Gulchenrouz cried out, and resisted till his cheeks became the colour of the blossom of the pomegranite, and the tears that started into his eyes shot forth a gleam of indignation. He cast a significant glance at Nouronihar, which the Caliph noticing, asked:

"Is that then your Gulchenrouz?"

"Sovereign of the world," answered she, "spare my cousin, whose innocence and gentleness deserve not your anger!"

"Take comfort," said Vathek with a smile, "he is in good hands. Bababalouk is fond of children, and never goes without sweetmeats and comfits."

The daughter of Fakreddin was abashed; and suffered Gulchenrouz to be borne away without adding a word. The tumult of her bosom betrayed her confusion; and Vathek becoming still more impassioned, gave a loose to his frenzy, which had only not subdued the last faint strugglings of reluctance, when the emir suddenly bursting in, threw his face upon the ground at the feet of the Caliph, and said:

"Commander of the faithful, abase not yourself to the meanness of your slave."

"No, emir," replied Vathek, "I raise her to an equality with myself; I declare her my wife; and the glory of your race shall extend from one generation to another."

"Alas! my lord," said Fakreddin, as he plucked off the honours of his beard, "cut short the days of your faithful servant rather than force him to depart from his word. Nouronihar, as her hands evince, is solemnly promised to Gulchenrouz, the son of my bother, Ali Hassan; they are united also in heart; their faith is mutually plighted; and affiances so sacred cannot be broken."

"What, then," replied the Caliph bluntly, "would you surrender this divine beauty to a husband more womanish than herself? And can you imagine that I will suffer her charms to decay in hands so inefficient and nerveless? No! she is destined to live out her life within my embraces: such is my will: retire, and disturb not the night I devote to the homage of her charms."

The irritated emir drew forth his sabre, presented it to Vathek, and stretching out his neck, said in a firm tone of voice:

"Strike your unhappy host my lord! he has lived long enough, since he hath seen the prophet's vicegerent violate the rights of hospitality."

At his uttering these words, Nouronihar unable to support any longer the conflict of her passions, sunk down in a swoon. Vathek, both terrified for her life, and furious at an opposition to his will, bade Fakreddin assist his daughter, and withdrew, darting his terrible look at the unfortunate emir, who suddenly fell backward bathed in a sweat, cold as the damp of death.

Gulchenrouz, who had escaped from the hands of Bababalouk, and was that instant returned, called out for help as loudly as he could, not having strength to afford it himself. Pale and panting, the poor child attempted to revive Nouronihar by caresses, and it happened that the thrilling warmth of his lips restored her to life. Fakreddin beginning also to recover from the look of the Caliph, with difficulty tottered to a seat, and after warily casting round his eye to see if this dangerous prince were gone, sent for Shaban and Sutlememe, and said to them apart—

"My friends, violent evils require as violent remedies; the Caliph has brought desolation and horror into my family, and how shall we resist his power? Another of his looks will send me to my grave. Fetch then that narcotic powder which the Dervise brought me from Aracan. A dose of it, the effect of which will continue three days, must be administered to each of these children. The Caliph will believe them to be dead, for they will have all the appearance of death. We shall go as if to inter them in the cave of Meimoune, at the entrance of the great desert of sand, and near the cabin of my dwarfs. When all the spectators shall be withdrawn, you, Shaban, and four select eunuchs shall convey them to the lake, where provision shall be ready to support them a month; for, one day allotted to the surprise this event will occasion, five to the tears, a fortnight to reflection, and the rest to prepare for renewing his progress, will, according to my calculation, fill up the whole time that Vathek will tarry, and I shall then be freed from his intrusion."

"Your plan," said Sutlememe, "is a good one, if it can but be effected. I have remarked that Nouronihar is well able to support the glances of the Caliph, and that he is far from being sparing of them to her; be assured therefore, notwithstanding her fondness for Gulchenrouz, she will never remain quiet while she knows him to be here, unless we can persuade her that both herself and Gulchenrouz are really dead, and that they were conveyed to those rocks for a limited season to expiate the little faults of which their love was the cause. We will add that we killed ourselves in despair, and that your dwarfs whom they never yet saw will preach to them delectable sermons. I will engage that every thing shall succeed to the bent of your wishes."

"Be it so," said Fakreddin; "I approve your proposal; let us lose not a moment to give it effect." They forthwith hastened to seek for the powder, which being mixed in a sherbet was immediately drunk by Gulchenrouz and Nouronihar. Within the space of an hour both were seized with violent palpitations, and a general numbness gradually ensued. They arose from the floor, where they had remained ever since the Caliph's departure, and ascending to the sofa, reclined themselves at full length upon it, clasped in each other's embraces.

"Cherish me, my dear Nouronihar," said Gulchenrouz; "put thy hand upon my heart, for it feels as if it were frozen. Alas! thou art as cold as myself! hath the Caliph murdered us both with his terrible look?"

"I am dying," cried she in a faltering voice; "press me closer, I am ready to expire!"

"Let us die then together," answered the little Gulchenrouz, whilst his breast laboured with a convulsive sigh; "let me at least breathe forth my soul on thy lips."

They spoke no more, and became as dead.

Immediately the most piercing cries were heard through the harem, whilst Shaban and Sutlememe personated with great adroitness the parts of persons in despair. The emir, who was sufficiently mortified to be forced into such untoward expedients, and had now for the first time made a trial of his powder, was under no necessity of counterfeiting grief. The slaves, who had flocked together from all quarters, stood motionless at the spectacle before them. All lights were extinguished save two lamps, which shed a wan glimmering over the faces of these lovely flowers, that seemed to be faded in the spring-time of life. Funeral vestments were prepared; their bodies were washed with rose water; their beautiful tresses were braided and incensed; and they were wrapped in symars whiter than alabaster. At the moment that their attendants were placing two wreaths of their favourite jasamines on their brows, the Caliph, who had just heard the tragical catastrophe, arrived. He looked not less pale and haggard than the goules that wander at night among graves. Forgetful of himself and every one else, he broke through the midst of the slaves, fell prostrate at the foot of the sofa, beat his bosom, called himself "atrocious murderer," and invoked upon his head a thousand imprecations. With a trembling hand he raised the veil that covered the countenance of Nouronihar, and uttering a loud shriek fell lifeless on the floor. The chief of the eunuchs dragged him off with horrible grimaces, and repeated as he went:

"Aye, I foresaw she would play you some ungracious turn."

No sooner was the Caliph gone than the emir commanded biers to be brought, and forbade that any one should enter the harem. Every window was fastened; all instruments of music were broken; and the Imams began to recite their prayers. Towards the close of this melancholy day Vathek sobbed in silence, for they had been forced to compose with anodynes his convulsions of rage and desperation.

At the dawn of the succeeding morning the wide folding doors of the palace were set open, and the funeral procession moved forward for the mountain. The wailful cries of "La Ilah illa Alla," reached to the Caliph, who was eager to cicatrize himself and attend the ceremonial; nor could he have been dissuaded, had not his excessive weakness disabled him from walking. At the few first steps he fell on the ground, and his people were obliged to lay him on a bed, where he remained many days in such a state of insensibility as excited compassion in the emir himself.

When the procession was arrived at the grot of Meimoune, Shaban and Sutlememe dismissed the whole of the train excepting the four confidential eunuchs who were appointed to remain. After resting some moments near the biers which had been left in the open air, they caused them to be carried to the brink of a small lake whose banks were overgrown with a hoary moss. This was the great resort of herons and storks, which preyed continually on little blue fishes. The dwarfs, instructed by the emir, soon repaired thither, and with the help of the eunuchs began to construct cabins of rushes and reeds, a work in which they had admirable skill. A magazine also was contrived for provisions, with a small oratory for themselves, and a pyramid of wood neatly piled, to furnish the necessary fuel, for the air was bleak in the hollows of the mountains.

At evening two fires were kindled on the brink of the lake, and the two lovely bodies taken from their biers were carefully deposited upon a bed of dried leaves within the same cabin. The dwarfs began to recite the koran with their clear shrill voices, and Shaban and Sutlememe stood at some distance anxiously waiting the effects of the powder. At length Nouronihar and Gulchenrouz faintly stretched out their arms, and gradually opening their eyes began to survey with looks of increasing amazement every object around them. They even attempted to rise, but for want of strength fell back again. Sutlememe on this administered a cordial which the emir had taken care to provide.

Gulchenrouz thoroughly aroused sneezed out aloud, and raising himself with an effort that expressed his surprise, left the cabin, and inhaled the fresh air with the greatest avidity.

"Yes," said he, "I breathe again! again do I exist! I hear sounds! I behold a firmament spangled over with stars!"

Nouronihar catching these beloved accents extricated herself from the leaves, and ran to clasp Gulchenrouz to her bosom. The first objects she remarked were their long symars, their garlands of flowers, and their naked feet: she hid her face in her hands to reflect. The vision of the enchanted bath, the despair of her father, and more vividly than both, the majestic figure of Vathek recurred to her memory. She recollected also, that herself and Gulchenrouz had been sick and dying; but all these images bewildered her mind. Not knowing where she was, she turned her eyes on all sides, as if to recognise the surrounding scene. This singular lake, those flames reflected from its glassy surface, the pale hues of its banks, the romantic cabins, the bull-rushes that sadly waved their drooping heads, the storks whose melancholy cries blended with the shrill voices of the dwarfs, every thing conspired to persuade them that the angel of death had opened the portal of some other world.

Gulchenrouz on his part, lost in wonder, clung to the neck of his cousin. He believed himself in the region of phantoms, and was terrified at the silence she preserved. At length addressing her:

"Speak," said he; "where are we! do you not see those spectres that are stirring the burning coals? Are they the Monker and Nakir, come to throw us into them? Does the fatal bridge cross this lake, whose solemn stillness perhaps conceals from us an abyss, in which for whole ages we shall be doomed incessantly to sink?"

"No my children," said Sutlememe going towards them; "take comfort, the exterminating angel who conducted our souls hither after yours, hath assured us that the chastisement of your indolent and voluptuous life shall be restricted to a certain series of years, which you must pass in this dreary abode, where the sun is scarcely visible, and where the soil yields neither fruits nor flowers. These," continued she, pointing to the dwarfs, "will provide for our wants; for souls so mundane as ours retain too strong a tincture of their earthly extraction. Instead of meats, your food will be nothing but rice, and your bread shall be moistened in the fogs that brood over the surface of the lake."

At this desolating prospect the poor children burst into tears, and prostrated themselves before the dwarfs, who perfectly supported their characters, and delivered an excellent discourse of a customary length upon the sacred camel, which after a thousand years was to convey them to the paradise of the faithful.

The sermon being ended and ablutions performed, they praised Alla and the prophet, supped very indifferently, and retired to their withered leaves. Nouronihar and her little cousin consoled themselves on finding that, though dead, they yet lay in one cabin. Having slept well before, the remainder of the night was spent in conversation on what had befallen them; and both, from a dread of apparitions, betook themselves for protection to one another's arms.

In the morning, which was lowering and rainy, the dwarfs mounted high poles like minarets, and called them to prayers. The whole congregation, which consisted of Sutlememe, Shaban, the four eunuchs, and some storks, were already assembled. The two children came forth from their cabin with a slow and dejected pace. As their minds were in a tender and melancholy mood, their devotions were performed with fervour. No sooner were they finished than Gulchenrouz demanded of Sutlememe and the rest, "how they happened to die so opportunely for his cousin and himself."

"We killed ourselves," returned Sutlememe, "in despair at your death."

On this, said Nouronihar, who notwithstanding what was past, had not yet forgotten her vision:

"And the Caliph, is he also dead of his grief? and will he likewise come hither?"

The dwarfs, who were prepared with an answer, most demurely replied:

"Vathek is damned beyond all redemption!"

"I readily believe so," said Gulchenrouz; "and am glad from my heart to hear it, for I am convinced it was his horrible look that sent us hither, to listen to sermons and mess upon rice."

One week passed away on the side of the lake unmarked by any variety; Nouronihar ruminating on the grandeur of which death had deprived her, and Gulchenrouz applying to prayers and to panniers along with the dwarfs, who infinitely pleased him. Whilst this scene of innocence was exhibiting in the mountains, the Caliph presented himself to the emir in a new light. The instant he recovered the use of his senses, with a voice that made Bababalouk quake, he thundered out:

"Perfidious Giaour! I renounce thee for ever! it is thou who hast slain my beloved Nouronihar! and I supplicate the pardon of Mahomet, who would have preserved her to me had I been more wise. Let water be brought to perform my ablutions, and let the pious Fakreddin be called to offer up his prayers with mine, and reconcile me to him. Afterwards we will go together and visit the sepulchre of the unfortunate Nouronihar. I am resolved to become a hermit, and consume the residue of my days on this mountain, in hope of expiating my crimes."

Nouronihar was not altogether so content, for though she felt a fondness for Gulchenrouz, who to augment the attachment, had been left at full liberty with her, yet she still regarded him as but a bauble that bore no competition with the carbuncle of Giamschid. At times she indulged doubts on the mode of her being, and scarcely could believe that the dead had all the wants and the whims of the living. To gain satisfaction, however, on so perplexing a topic, she arose one morning whilst all were asleep with a breathless caution from the side of Gulchenrouz, and after having given him a soft kiss, began to follow the windings of the lake till it terminated with a rock whose top was accessible though lofty. This she clambered up with considerable toil, and having reached the summit, set forward in a run like a doe that unwittingly follows her hunter. Though she skipped along with the alertness of an antelope, yet at intervals she was forced to desist, and rest beneath the tamarisks to recover her breath. Whilst she, thus reclined, was occupied with her little reflections on the apprehension that she had some knowledge of the place, Vathek, who finding himself that morning but ill at ease, had gone forth before the dawn, presented himself on a sudden to her view. Motionless with surprise, he durst not approach the figure before him, which lay shrouded up in a symar extended on the ground, trembling and pale, but yet lovely to behold. At length Nouronihar, with a mixture of pleasure and affliction, raising her fine eyes to him, said:

"My lord, are you come hither to eat rice and hear sermons with me?"

"Beloved phantom!" cried Vathek, "dost thou speak? hast thou the same graceful form? the same radiant features? art thou palpable likewise?" and eagerly embracing her he added, "here are limbs and a bosom animated with a gentle warmth! what can such a prodigy mean?"

Nouronihar with diffidence answered:

"You know my lord that I died on the night you honoured me with your visit; my cousin maintains it was from one of your glances, but I cannot believe him, for to me they seem not so dreadful. Gulchenrouz died with me, and we were both brought into a region of desolation, where we are fed with a wretched diet. If you be dead also, and are come hither to join us, I pity your lot, for you will be stunned with the clang of the dwarfs and the storks. Besides, it is mortifying in the extreme that you as well as myself should have lost the treasures of the subterranean palace."

At the mention of the subterranean palace, the Caliph suspended his caresses, which indeed had proceeded pretty far, to seek from Nouronihar an explanation of her meaning. She then recapitulated her vision — what immediately followed — and the history of her pretended death; adding also a description of the palace of expiation from whence she had fled; and all in a manner that would have extorted his laughter, had not the thoughts of Vathek been too deeply engaged. No sooner, however, had she ended, than he again clasped her to his bosom, and said:

"Light of my eyes! the mystery is unravelled; we both are alive! Your father is a cheat, who for the sake of dividing hath deluded us both; and the Giaour, whose design, as far as I can discover, is that we shall proceed together, seems scarce a whit better. It shall be some time at least before he find us in his palace of fire. Your lovely little person in my estimation is far more precious than all the treasures of the preadimite sultans, and I wish to possess it at pleasure, and in open day for many a moon, before I go to burrow under ground like a mole."

"Forget this little trifler Gulchenrouz, and" —

"Ah, my lord," interposed Nouronihar, "let me entreat that you do him no evil."

"No, no," replied Vathek, "I have already bid you forbear to alarm yourself for him. He has been brought up too much on milk and sugar to stimulate my jealousy. We will leave him with the dwarfs, who by the bye are my old acquaintances; their company will suit him far better than yours. As to other matters, I will return no more to your father's. I want not to have my ears dinned by him and his dotards with the violation of the rights of hospitality; as if it were less an honour for you to espouse the sovereign of the world, than a girl dressed up like a boy."

Nouronihar could find nothing to oppose in a discourse so eloquent. She only wished the amorous monarch had discovered more ardour for the carbuncle of Giamschid; but flattered herself it would gradually increase, and therefore yielded to his will with the most bewitching submission.

When the Caliph judged it proper he called for Bababalouk, who was asleep in the cave of Meimoune, and dreaming that the phantom of Nouronihar having mounted him once more on her swing, had just given him such a jerk that he one moment soared above the mountains, and the next sunk into the abyss. Starting from his sleep at the voice of his master, he ran gasping for breath, and had nearly fallen backward at the sight, as he believed, of the spectre, by whom he had so lately been haunted in his dream.

"Ah my lord," cried he, recoiling ten steps, and covering his eyes with both hands, "do you then perform the office of a goule? 'Tis true you have dug up the dead, yet hope not to make her your prey; for after all she hath caused me to suffer, she is even wicked enough to prey upon you."

"Cease thy folly," said Vathek, "and thou shalt soon be convinced that it is Nouronihar herself, alive and well, whom I clasp to my breast. Go only, and pitch my tents in the neighbouring valley. There will I fix my abode with this beautiful tulip, whose colours I soon shall restore. There exert thy best endeavours to procure whatever can augment the enjoyments of life, till I shall disclose to thee more of my will."

The news of so unlucky an event soon reached the ears of the emir, who abandoned himself to grief and despair, and began, as did all his old greybeards, to begrime his visage with ashes. A total supineness ensued; travellers were no longer entertained, no more plasters were spread, and instead of the charitable activity that had distinguished this asylum, the whole of its inhabitants exhibited only faces of a half cubit long, and uttered groans that accorded with their forlorn situation.

Though Fakreddin bewailed his daughter as lost to him for ever, yet Gulchenrouz was not forgotten. He despatched immediate instruction to Sutlememe, Shaban, and the dwarfs, enjoining them not to undeceive the child in respect to his state, but under some pretence to convey him far from the lofty rock at the extremity of the lake, to a place which he should appoint, as safer from danger; for he suspected that Vathek intended him evil.

Gulchenrouz in the mean while was filled with amazement at not finding his cousin; nor were the dwarfs at all less surprised; but Sutlememe, who had more penetration, immediately guessed what had happened. Gulchenrouz was amused with the delusive hope of once more embracing Nouronihar in the interior recesses of the mountains, where the ground, strewed over with orange blossoms and jasamines, offered beds much more inviting than the withered leaves in their cabin, where they might accompany with their voices the sounds of their lutes, and chase butterflies in concert. Sutlememe was far gone in this sort of description when one of the four eunuchs beckoned her aside to apprise her of the arrival of a messenger from their fraternity, who had explained the secret of the flight of Nouronihar, and brought the commands of the emir. A council with Shaban and the dwarfs was immediately held. Their baggage being stowed in consequence of it, they embarked in a shallop and quietly sailed with the little one, who acquiesced in all their proposals. Their voyage proceeded in the same manner, till they came to the place where the lake sinks beneath the hollow of the rock, but as soon as the bark had entered it, and Gulchenrouz found himself surrounded with darkness, he was seized with a dreadful consternation, and incessantly uttered the most piercing outcries; for he now was persuaded he should actually be damned for having taken too many little freedoms in his life-time with his cousin.

But let us return to the Caliph, and her who ruled over his heart. Bababalouk had pitched the tents, and closed up the extremities of the valley with magnificent screens of India cloth, which were guarded by Ethiopian slaves with their drawn sabres. To preserve the verdure of this beautiful enclosure in its natural freshness, the white eunuchs went continually round it with their red water vessels. The waving of fans was heard near the imperial pavilion, where by the voluptuous light that glowed through the muslins, the Caliph enjoyed at full view all the attractions of Nouronihar. Inebriated with delight, he was all ear to her charming voice which accompanied the lute; while she was not less captivated with his descriptions of Samarah and the tower full of wonders, but especially with his relation of the adventure of the ball, and the chasm of the Giaour with its ebony portal.

In this manner they conversed for a day and a night; they bathed together in a basin of black marble, which admirably relieved the fairness of Nouronihar. Bababalouk, whose good graces this beauty had regained, spared no attention that their repasts might be served up with the minutest exactness: some exquisite rariety was ever placed before them; and he sent even to Schiraz for that fragrant and delicious wine which had been hoarded up in bottles prior to the birth of Mahomet. He had excavated little ovens in the rock to bake the nice manchets which were prepared by the hands of Nouronihar, from whence they had derived a flavour so grateful to Vathek, that he regarded the ragouts of his other wives as entirely maukish; whilst they would have died at the emir's of chagrin at finding themselves so neglected, if Fakreddin, notwithstanding his resentment, had not taken pity upon them.

The sultana Dilara, who till then had been the favourite, took this dereliction of the Caliph to heart with a vehemence natural to her character; for during her continuance in favour she had imbibed from Vathek many of his extravagant fancies, and was fired with impatience to behold the superb tombs of Istakar, and the palace of forty columns; besides, having been brought up amongst the magi, she had fondly cherished the idea of the Caliph's devoting himself to the worship of fire; thus his voluptuous and desultory life with her rival was to her a double source of affliction. The transient piety of Vathek had occasioned her some serious alarms, but the present was an evil of far greater magnitude. She resolved therefore without hesitation to write to Carathis, and acquaint her that all things went ill; that they had eaten, slept, and revelled at an old emir's, whose sanctity was very formidable, and that after all the prospect of possessing the treasures of the preadimite sultans was no less remote than before. This letter was entrusted to the care of two woodmen who were at work on one of the great forests of the mountains, and being acquainted with the shortest cuts, arrived in ten days at Samarah.

The princess Carathis was engaged at chess with Morakanabad, when the arrival of these wood-fellers was announced. She, after some weeks of Vathek's absence, had forsaken the upper regions of her tower, because everything appeared in confusion among the stars, whom she consulted relative to the fate of her son. In vain did she renew her fumigations, and extend herself on the roof to obtain mystic visions, nothing more could she see in her dreams than pieces of brocade, nosegays of flowers, and other unmeaning gewgaws. These disappointments had thrown her into a state of dejection which no drug in her power was sufficient to remove. Her only resource was in Morakanabad, who was a good man, and endowed with a decent share of confidence, yet whilst in her company he never thought himself on roses.

No person knew aught of Vathek, and a thousand ridiculous stories were propagated at his expense. The eagerness of Carathis may be easily guessed at receiving the letter, as well as her rage at reading the dissolute conduct of her son.

"Is it so," said she; "either I will perish, or Vathek shall enter the palace of fire. Let me expire in flames, provided he may reign on the throne of Soliman!"

Having said this, and whirled herself round in a magical manner, which struck Morakanabad with such terror as caused him to recoil, she ordered her great camel Alboufaki to be brought, and the hideous Nerkes with the unrelenting Cafour to attend.

"I require no other retinue," said she to Morakanabad: "I am going on affairs of emergency, a truce therefore to parade! Take you care of the people, fleece them well in my absence, for we shall expend large sums, and one knows not what may betide."

The night was uncommonly dark, and a pestilential blast ravaged the plain of Catoul that would have deterred any other traveller however urgent the call; but Carathis enjoyed most whatever filled others with dread. Nerkes concurred in opinion with her, and Cafour had a particular predilection for a pestilence. In the morning this accomplished caravan, with the wood-fellers who directed their route, halted on the edge of an extensive marsh, from whence so noxious a vapour arose as would have destroyed any animal but Alboufaki, who naturally inhaled these malignant fogs. The peasants entreated their convoy not to sleep in this place.

"To sleep," cried Carathis, "what an excellent thought! I never sleep but for visions; and as to my attendants, their occupations are too many to close the only eye they each have."

The poor peasants, who were not over pleased with their party, remained open-mouthed with surprise.

Carathis alighted as well as her negresses, and severally stripping off their outer garments, they all ran in their drawers to cull from those spots where the sun shone fiercest, the venomous plants that grew on the marsh. This provision was made for the family of the emir, and whoever might retard the expedition to Istakar. The woodmen were overcome with fear when they beheld these three horrible phantoms run, and not much relishing the company of Alboufaki, stood aghast at the command of Carathis to set forward, notwithstanding it was noon, and the heat fierce enough to calcine even rocks. In spite, however, of every remonstrance, they were forced implicitly to submit.

Alboufaki, who delighted in solitude, constantly snorted whenever he perceived himself near a habitation, and Carathis, who was apt to spoil him with indulgence, as constantly turned him aside; so that the peasants were precluded from procuring subsistence; for the milch goats and ewes which Providence had sent towards the district they traversed, to refresh travellers with their milk, all fled at the sight of the hideous animal and his strange riders. As to Carathis, she needed no common aliment; for her invention had previously furnished her with an opiate to stay her stomach, some of which she imparted to her mutes.

At the fall of night Alboufaki making a sudden stop, stamped with his foot, which to Carathis, who understood his paces, was a certain indication that she was near the confines of some cemetery. The moon shed a bright light on the spot, which served to discover a long wall with a large door in it standing a-jar, and so high that Alboufaki might easily enter. The miserable guides, who perceived their end approaching, humbly implored Carathis, as she had now so good an opportunity, to inter them, and immediately gave up the ghost. Nerkes and Cafour, whose wit was of a style peculiar to themselves, were by no means parsimonious of it on the folly of these poor people, nor could any thing have been found more suited to their taste than the site of the burying ground, and the sepulchres which its precincts contained. There were at least two thousand of them on the declivity of a hill; some in the form of pyramids, others like columns, and in short the variety of their shapes was endless. Carathis was too much immersed in her sublime contemplations to stop at the view, charming as it appeared in her eyes. Pondering the advantages that might accrue from her present situation, she could not forbear to exclaim:

"So beautiful a cemetery must be haunted by Gouls, and they want not for intelligence! having heedlessly suffered my guides to expire, I will apply for directions to them, and as an inducement, will invite them to regale on these fresh corpses."

After this short soliloquy, she beckoned to Nerkes and Cafour, and made signs with her fingers, as much as to say:

"Go, knock against the sides of the tombs, and strike up your delightful warblings, that are so like to those of the guests whose company I wish to obtain."

The negresses, full of joy at the behests of their mistress, and promising themselves much pleasure from the society of the Gouls, went with an air of conquest, and began their knockings at the tombs. As their strokes were repeated, a hollow noise was heard in the earth, the surface hove up into heaps, and the Gouls on all sides protruded their noses to inhale the effluvia which the carcasses of the woodmen began to emit.

They assembled before a sarcophagus of white marble, where Carathis was seated between the bodies of her miserable guides. The princess received her visitants with distinguished politeness, and when supper was ended, proceeded with them to business. Having soon learnt from them every thing she wished to discover, it was her intention to set forward forthwith on her journey, but her negresses, who were forming tender connections with the Gouls, importuned her with all their fingers to wait, at least till the dawn. Carathis, however, being chastity in the abstract, and an implacable enemy to love and repose, at once rejected their prayer, mounted Alboufaki, and commanded them to take their seats in a moment. Four days and four nights she continued her route, without turning to the right hand or left; on the fifth she traversed the mountains and half-burnt forests, and arrived on the sixth before the beautiful screens which concealed from all eyes the voluptuous wanderings of her son.

It was day-break, and the guards were snoring on their posts in careless security, when the rough trot of Alboufaki awoke them in consternation. Imagining that a group of spectres ascended from the abyss was approaching, they all without ceremony took to their heels. Vathek was at that instant with Nouronihar in the bath, hearing tales and laughing at Bababalouk who related them; but no sooner did the outcry of his guards reach him, than he flounced from the water like a carp, and as soon threw himself back at the sight of Carathis, who advancing with her negresses upon Alboufaki, broke through the muslin awnings and veils of the pavilion. At this sudden apparition Nouronihar (for she was not at all times free from remorse) fancied that the moment of celestial vengeance was come, and clung about the Caliph in amorous despondence.

Carathis, still seated on her camel, foamed with indignation at the spectacle which obtruded itself on her chaste view. She thundered forth without check or mercy:

"Thou double-headed and four legged monster! what means all this winding and writhing? art thou not ashamed to be seen grasping this limber sapling, in preference to the sceptre of the preadimite sultans? Is it then for this paltry doxy that thou hast violated the conditions in the parchment of our Giaour? Is it on her thou hast lavished thy precious moments? Is this the fruit of the knowledge I have taught thee? Is this the end of thy journey? Tear thyself from the arms of this little simpleton; drown her in the water before me, and instantly follow my guidance."

In the first ebullition of his fury, Vathek resolved to make a skeleton of Alboufaki, and to stuff the skins of Carathis and her blacks; but the ideas of the Giaour, the palace of Istakar, the sabres, and the talismans, flashing before his imagination with the simultaneousness of lightning, he became more moderate, and said to his mother in a civil but decisive tone:

"Dread lady, you shall be obeyed; but I will not drown Nouronihar; she is sweeter to me than a Myrabolan comfit, and is enamoured of carbuncles, especially that of Giamschid, which hath also been promised to be conferred upon her; she therefore shall go along with us, for I intend to repose with her beneath the canopies of Soliman; I can sleep no more without her."

"Be it so," replied Carathis alighting, and at the same time committing Alboufaki to the charge of her women.

Nouronihar, who had not yet quitted her hold, began to take courage, and said with an accent of fondness to the Caliph:

"Dear sovereign of my soul! I will follow thee, if it be thy will beyond the Kaf, in the land of the Afrits. I will not hesitate to climb for thee the nest of the Simurgh, who, this lady excepted, is the most awful of created existences."

"We have here then," subjoined Carathis, "a girl both of courage and science."

Nouronihar had certainly both; but notwithstanding all her firmness, she could not help casting back a look of regret upon the graces of her little Gulchenrouz, and the days of tenderness she had participated with him. She even dropped a few tears, which Carathis observed, and inadvertently breathed out with a sigh:

"Alas! my gentle cousin, what will become of him!"

Vathek at this apostrophe knitted up his brows, and Carathis enquired what it could mean.

"She is preposterously sighing after a stripling with languishing eyes and soft hair who loves her," said the Caliph.

"Where is he?" asked Carathis. "I must be acquainted with this pretty child; for," added she, lowering her voice, "I design before I depart to regain the favour of the Giaour. There is nothing so delicious in his estimation as the heart of a delicate boy, palpitating with the first tumults of love."

Vathek as he came from the bath commanded Bababalouk to collect the women and other moveables of his harem, embody his troops, and hold himself in readiness to march in three days; whilst Carathis retired alone to a tent, where the Giaour solaced her with encouraging visions; but at length waking, she found at her feet Nerkes and Cafour, who informed her by their signs, that having led Alboufaki to the borders of a lake, to browse on some moss that looked tolerably venomous, they had discovered certain blue fishes of the same kind with those in the reservoir on the top of the tower.

"Ah, ah," said she, "I will go thither to them. These fish are past doubt of a species that by a small operation I can render oracular. They may tell me where this little Gulchenrouz is, whom I am bent upon sacrificing."

Having thus spoken, she immediately set out with her swarthy retinue.

It being but seldom that time is lost in the accomplishment of a wicked enterprise, Carathis and her negresses soon arrived at the lake, where, after burning the magical drugs with which they were always provided, they, stripping themselves naked, waded to their chins, Nerkes and Cafour waving torches around them, and Carathis pronouncing her barbarous incantations. The fishes with one accord thrust forth their heads from the water, which was violently rippled by the flutter of their fins, and at length finding themselves constrained by the potency of the charm, they opened their piteous mouths, said:

"From gills to tail we are yours; what seek ye to know?"

"Fishes," answered she, "I conjure you by your glittering scales, tell me where now is Gulchenrouz?"

"Beyond the rock," replied the shoal in full chorus: "will this content you? for we do not delight in expanding our mouths."

"It will," returned the princess: "I am not to learn that you like not long conversations; I will leave you therefore to repose, though I had other questions to propound."

The instant she had spoken the water became smooth, and the fishes at once disappeared.

Carathis, inflated with the venom of her projects, strode hastily over the rock, and found the amiable Gulchenrouz asleep in an arbour, whilst the two dwarfs were watching at his side, and ruminating their accustomed prayers. These diminutive personages possessed the gift of divining whenever an enemy to good Mussulmans approached; thus they anticipated the arrival of Carathis, who stopping short, said to herself:

"How placidly doth he recline his lovely little head! how pale and languishing are his looks! it is just the very child of my wishes!"

The dwarfs interrupted this delectable soliloquy by leaping instantly upon her, and scratching her face with their utmost zeal. But Nerkes and Cafour betaking themselves to the succour of their mistress, pinched the dwarfs so severely in return, that they both gave up the ghost, imploring Mahomet to inflict his sorest vengeance upon this wicked woman and all her household.

At the noise which this strange conflict occasioned in the valley, Gulchenrouz awoke, and bewildered with terror sprung impetuously upon an old fig-tree that rose against the acclivity of the rocks, from thence gained their summits, and ran for two hours without once looking back. At last, exhausted with fatigue, he fell as if dead into the arms of a good old Genius, whose fondness for the company of children had made it his sole occupation to protect them, and who, whilst performing his wonted rounds through the air, happening on the cruel Giaour at the instant of his growling in the horrible chasm, rescued the fifty little victims which the impiety of Vathek had devoted to his maw. These the Genius brought up in nests still higher than the clouds, and himself fixed his abode in a nest more capacious than the rest, from which he had expelled the possessors that had built it.

These inviolable asylums were defended against the Dives and the Afrits by waving streamers, on which were inscribed in characters of gold that flashed like lightning, the names of Alla and the prophet. It was there that Gulchenrouz, who as yet remained undeceived with respect to his pretended death, thought himself in the mansions of eternal peace. He admitted without fear the congratulations of his little friends, who were all assembled in the nest of the venerable Genius, and vied with each other in kissing his serene forehead and beautiful eye-lids. This he found to be the state congenial to his soul—remote from the inquietudes of earth—the impertinence of harems—the brutality of eunuchs—and the lubricity of women. In this peaceable society his days, months, and years glided on, nor was he less happy than the rest of his companions, for the Genius, instead of burdening his pupils with perishable riches, and the vain sciences of the world, conferred upon them the boon of perpetual childhood.

Carathis, unaccustomed to the loss of her prey, vented a thousand execrations on her negresses for not seizing the child, instead of amusing themselves with pinching to death the dwarfs, from which they could gain no advantage. She returned into the valley murmuring, and finding that her son was not risen from the arms of Nouronihar, discharged her ill-humour upon both. The idea, however, of departing next day for Istakar, and cultivating, through the good offices of the Giaour, an intimacy with Eblis himself, at length consoled her chagrin: but fate had ordained it otherwise.

In the evening, as Carathis was conversing with Dilara, who through her contrivance had become of the party, and whose taste resembled her own, Bababalouk came to acquaint her "that the sky towards Samarah looked of a fiery red, and seemed to portend some alarming disaster." Immediately recurring to her astrolabes and instruments of magic, she took the altitude of the planets, and discovered by her calculations, to her great mortification, that a formidable revolt had taken place at Samarah; that Motavakel, availing himself of the disgust which was inveterate against his brother had incited commotions amongst the populace, made himself master of the palace, and actually invested the great tower, to which Morakanabad had retired with a handful of the few that still remained faithful to Vathek.

"What," exclaimed she, "must I lose then my tower, my mutes, my negresses, my mummies, and worse than all, the laboratory, in which I have spent so many a night, without knowing, at least, if my hair-brained son will complete his adventure? No! I will not be the dupe! Immediately will I speed to support Morakanabad. By my formidable art the clouds shall sleet hail-stones in the faces of the assailants, and shafts of red-hot iron on their heads. I will spring mines of serpents and torpedoes from beneath them, and we shall soon see the stand they will make against such an explosion!"

Having thus spoken, Carathis hasted to her son, who was tranquilly banqueting with Nouronihar in his superb carnation coloured tent.

"Glutton that thou art," cried she, "were it not for me, thou wouldst soon find thyself the commander only of pies. Thy faithful subjects have abjured the faith they swore to thee. Motavakel thy brother now reigns on the hill of pied horses; and had I not some slight resources in the tower, would not be easily persuaded to abdicate. But that time may not be lost, I shall only add four words: strike tent to-night; set forward; and beware how thou loiterest again by the way. Though thou hast forfeited the conditions of the parchment, I am not yet without hope; for it cannot be denied that thou hast violated to admiration the laws of hospitality by seducing the daughter of the emir, after having partaken of his bread and his salt. Such a conduct cannot but be delightful to the Giaour; and if on thy march thou canst signalize thyself by an additional crime, all will still go well, and thou shalt enter the palace of Soliman in triumph. Adieu! Alboufaki and my negresses are waiting."

The Caliph had nothing to offer in reply: he wished his mother a prosperous journey, and eat on till he had finished his supper. At midnight the camp broke up, amidst the flourishing of trumpets and other martial instruments; but loud indeed must have been the sound of the tymbals, to overpower the blubbering of the emir and his long-beards, who by an excessive profusion of tears had so far exhausted the radical moisture, that their eyes shrivelled up in their sockets, and their hairs dropped off by the roots. Nouronihar, to whom such a symphony was painful, did not grieve to get out of hearing. She accompanied the Caliph in the imperial litter, where they amused themselves with imagining the splendour which was soon to surround them. The other women, overcome with dejection, were dolefully rocked in their cages, whilst Dilara consoled herself with anticipating the joy of celebrating the rites of fire on the stately terraces of Istakar.

In four days they reached the spacious valley of Rocnabad. The season of spring was in all its vigour, and the grotesque branches of the almond trees in full blossom fantastically chequered the clear blue sky. The earth, variegated with hyacinths and jonquils, breathed forth a fragrance which diffused through the soul a divine repose. Myriads of bees, and scarce fewer of Santons had there taken up their abode. On the banks of the stream hives and oratories were alternately ranged, and their neatness and whiteness were set off by the deep green of the cypresses that spired up amongst them. These pious personages amused themselves with cultivating little gardens that abounded with flowers and fruits, especially musk-melons of the best flavour that Persia could boast. Sometimes dispersed over the meadow they entertained themselves with feeding peacocks whiter than snow, and turtles more blue than the sapphire. In this manner were they occupied when the harbingers of the imperial procession began to proclaim:

"Inhabitants of Rocnabad, prostrate yourselves on the brink of your pure waters, and tender your thanksgivings to heaven that vouchsafeth to shew you a ray of its glory; for lo! the commander of the faithful draws near."

The poor Santons, filled with holy energy, having bustled to light up wax torches in their oratories, and expand the koran on their ebony desks, went forth to meet the Caliph with baskets of honeycomb, dates, and melons. But whilst they were advancing in solemn procession and with measured steps, the horses, camels, and guards wantoned over their tulips and other flowers, and made a terrible havoc amongst them. The Santons could not help casting from one eye a look of pity on the ravages committing around them, whilst the other was fixed upon the Caliph and heaven. Nouronihar, enraptured with the scenery of a place which brought back to her remembrance the pleasing solitudes where her infancy had passed, entreated Vathek to stop, but he, suspecting that each oratory might be deemed by the Giaour a distinct habitation, commanded his pioneers to level them all. The Santons stood motionless with horror at the barbarous mandate, and at last broke out into lamentations, but these were uttered with so ill a grace, that Vathek bade his eunuchs to kick them from his presence. He then descended from the litter with Nouronihar. They sauntered together in the meadow, and amused themselves with culling flowers, and passing a thousand pleasantries on each other. But the bees, who were staunch Mussulmans, thinking it their duty to revenge the insult on their dear masters the Santons, assembled so zealously to do it with effect, that the Caliph and Nouronihar were glad to find their tents prepared to receive them.

Bababalouk, who in capacity of purveyor, had acquitted himself with applause, as to peacocks and turtles, lost no time in consigning some dozens to the spit, and as many more to be fricasseed. Whilst they were feasting, laughing, carousing, and blaspheming at pleasure on the banquet so liberally furnished, the Moullahs, the Sheiks, the Cadis, and Imans of Schiraz (who seemed not to have met the Santons) arrived, leading by bridles of ribband, inscribed from the koran, a train of asses which were loaded with the choicest fruits the country could boast. Having presented their offerings to the Caliph, they petitioned him to honour their city and mosques with his presence.

"Fancy not," said Vathek, "that you can detain me. Your presents I condescend to accept, but beg you will let me be quiet, for I am not over fond of resisting temptation. Retire then. Yet, as it is not decent for personages so reverend to return on foot, and as you have not the appearance of expert riders, my eunuchs shall tie you on your asses with the precaution that your backs be not turned towards me, for they understand etiquette."

In this deputation were some high-stomached Sheiks, who taking Vathek for a fool, scrupled not to speak their opinion. These Bababalouk girded with double cords; and having well disciplined their asses with nettles behind, they all started with a preternatural alertness, plunging, kicking, and running foul of each other in the most ludicrous manner imaginable.

Nouronihar and the Caliph mutually contended who should most enjoy so degrading a sight. They burst out in volleys of laughter to see the old men and their asses fall into the stream. The leg of one was fractured, the shoulder of another dislocated, the teeth of a third dashed out, and the rest suffered still worse.

Two days more, undisturbed by fresh embassies, having been devoted to the pleasures of Rocnabad, the expedition proceeded, leaving Schiraz on the right, and verging towards a large plain, from whence were discernible on the edge of the horizon the dark summits of the mountains of Istakar.

At this prospect the Caliph and Nouronihar were unable to repress their transports. They bounded from their litter to the ground, and broke forth into such wild exclamations as amazed all within hearing. Interrogating each other, they shouted,

"Are we not approaching the radiant palace of light, or gardens more delightful than those of Sheddad?"

Infatuated mortals! they thus indulged delusive conjecture, unable to fathom the decrees of the Most High!

The good Genii who had not totally relinquished the superintendence of Vathek, repairing to Mahomet in the seventh heaven, said:

"Merciful Prophet! stretch forth thy propitious arms towards thy vicegerent, who is ready to fall irretrievably into the snare which his enemies the Dives have prepared to destroy him. The Giaour is awaiting his arrival in the abominable palace of fire, where if he once set his foot his perdition will be inevitable."

Mahomet answered with an air of indignation:

"He hath too well deserved to be resigned to himself; but I permit you to try if one effort more will be effectual to divert him from pursuing his ruin."

One of these beneficent Genii, assuming without delay the exterior of a shepherd, more renowned for his piety than all the Dervises and Santons of the region, took his station near a flock of white sheep on the slope of a hill, and began to pour forth from his flute such airs of pathetic melody, as subdued the very soul; and awakening remorse, drove far from it every frivolous fancy. At these energetic sounds, the sun hid himself beneath a gloomy cloud; and the waters of two little lakes, that were naturally clearer than chrystal, became a colour like blood. The whole of this superb assembly, was involuntarily drawn towards the declivity of the hill. With downcast eyes, they all stood abashed; each upbraiding himself with the evil he had done. The heart of Dilara palpitated; and the chief of the eunuchs, with a sigh of contrition, implored pardon of the women, whom, for his own satisfaction, he had so often tormented.

Vathek and Nouronihar turned pale in their litter; and, regarding each other with haggard looks, reproached themselves—the one with a thousand of the blackest crimes, a thousand projects of impious ambition; the other, with the desolation of her family, and the perdition of the amiable Gulchenrouz. Nouronihar persuaded herself that she heard in the fatal music the groans of her dying father; and Vathek, the sobs of the fifty children he had sacrificed to the Giaour. Amidst these complicated pangs of anguish, they perceived themselves impelled towards the shepherd, whose countenance was so commanding, that Vathek, for the first time, felt overawed; whilst Nouronihar concealed her face with her hands. The music paused, and the Genius, addressing the Caliph, said:

"Deluded Prince! to whom Providence hath confided the care of innumerable subjects, is it thus that thou fulfillest thy mission? Thy crimes are already completed; and, art thou now hastening towards thy punishment? Thou knowest, that beyond these mountains, Eblis and his accursed Dives hold their infernal empire; and seduced by a malignant phantom, thou art proceeding to surrender thyself to them! This moment is the last of grace allowed thee! Abandon thy atrocious purpose. Return. Give back Nouronihar to her father, who still retains a few sparks of life. Destroy thy tower, with all its abominations. Drive Carathis from thy councils. Be just to thy subjects. Respect the ministers of the Prophet. Compensate for thy impieties by an exemplary life; and, instead of squandering thy days in voluptuous indulgence, lament thy crimes on the sepulchres of thy ancestors. Thou beholdest the clouds that obscure the sun; at the instant he recovers his splendour, if thy heart be not changed, the time of mercy assigned thee will be past for ever."

Vathek, depressed with fear, was on the point of prostrating himself at the feet of the shepherd, whom he perceived to be of a nature superior to man, but his pride prevailing, he audaciously lifted his head, and glancing at him one of his terrible looks, said:

"Whoever thou art, withhold thy useless admonitions. Thou wouldst either delude me, or art thyself deceived. If what I have done be so criminal as thou pretendest, there remains not for me a moment of grace. I have traversed a sea of blood, to acquire a power which will make thy equals tremble; deem not that I shall retire when in view of the port; or that I will relinquish her who is dearer to me than either my life or thy mercy. Let the sun appear! Let him illumine my career! It matters not where it may end."

On uttering these words, which made even the Genius shudder, Vathek threw himself into the arms of Nouronihar, and commanded that his horses should be forced back to the road.

There was no difficulty in obeying these orders, for the attraction had ceased, the sun shone forth in all his glory, and the shepherd vanished with a lamentable scream.

The fatal impression of the music of the Genius remained, notwithstanding, in the hearts of Vathek's attendants. They viewed each other with looks of consternation. At the approach of night, almost all of them escaped; and, of this numerous assemblage, there only remained the chief of the eunuchs, some idolatrous slaves, Dilara, and a few other women, who, like herself, were votaries of the religion of the Magi.

The Caliph, fired with the ambition of prescribing laws to the Intelligences of Darkness, was but little embarrassed at this dereliction. The impetuosity of his blood prevented him from sleeping; nor did he encamp any more as before. Nouronihar, whose impatience, if possible, exceeded his own, importuned him to hasten his march, and lavished on him a thousand caresses, to beguile all reflection. She fancied herself already more potent than Balkis;[25] and pictured to her imagination the Genii falling prostrate at the foot of her throne. In this manner they advanced by moonlight, till they came within view of the two towering rocks, that form a kind of portal to the valley, at whose extremity rose the vast ruins of Istakar. Aloft on the mountain, glimmered the fronts of various royal mausoleums, the horror of which was deepened by the shadows of night. They passed through two villages, almost deserted; the only inhabitants remaining being a few feeble old men, who at the sight of horses and litters fell upon their knees, and cried out:

"O heaven! is it then by these phantoms that we have been for six months

---

[25] *Balkis.* This was the Arabian name of the Queen of Sheba, who went from the South to hear the wisdom and admire the glory of Solomon. The Koran represents her as a worshipper of fire. Solomon is said not only to have entertained her with the greatest magnificence, but also to have raised her to his bed and his throne. Al Koran, ch. 27, and Sale's notes. Herbelot, p. 182.

tormented! Alas! it was from the terror of these spectres, and the noise beneath the mountains, that our people have fled, and left us at the mercy of maleficent spirits!"

The Caliph, to whom these complaints were but unpromising auguries, drove over the bodies of these wretched old men, and at length arrived at the foot of the terrace of black marble. There he descended from his litter, handing down Nouronihar; both, with beating hearts, stared wildly around them, and expected, with an apprehensive shudder, the approach of the Giaour. But nothing as yet announced his appearance.

A deathlike stillness reigned over the mountain, and through the air. The moon dilated, on a vast platform, the shades of the lofty columns, which reached from the terrace almost to the clouds. The gloomy watch-towers, whose number could not be counted, were veiled by no roof: and their capitals, of an architecture unknown in the records of the earth, served as an asylum for the birds of darkness, which, alarmed at the approach of such visitants, fled away croaking.

The chief of the eunuchs, trembling with fear, besought Vathek that a fire might be kindled.

"No!" replied he, "there is no time left to think of such trifles; abide where thou art, and expect my commands."

Having thus spoken, he presented his hand to Nouronihar, and ascending the steps of a vast staircase, reached the terrace, which was flagged with squares of marble, and resembled a smooth expanse of water, upon whose surface not a leaf ever dared to vegetate. On the right rose the watch-towers, ranged before the ruins of an immense palace, whose walls were embossed with various figures. In front stood forth the colossal forms of four creatures, composed of the leopard and the griffin; and though but of stone, inspired emotions of terror. Near these were distinguished by the splendour of the moon, which streamed full on the place, characters like those on the sabres of the Giaour, that possessed the same virtue of changing every moment. These, after vacillating for some time, at last fixed in Arabic letters, and prescribed to the Caliph the following words:

"Vathek! thou hast violated the conditions of my parchment, and deservest to be sent back; but in favour to thy companion, and as the meed for what thou hast done to obtain it, Eblis permitteth that the portal of his palace shall be opened, and the subterranean fire will receive thee into the number of its adorers."

He scarcely had read these words before the mountain, against which the terrace was reared, trembled; and the watch-towers were ready to topple headlong upon them. The rock yawned, and disclosed within it a staircase of polished marble, that seemed to approach the abyss. Upon each stair were planted two large torches, like those Nouronihar had seen in her vision, the camphorated vapour ascending from which gathered into a cloud under the hollow of the vault.

This appearance, instead of terrifying, gave new courage to the daughter of Fakreddin. Scarcely deigning to bid adieu to the moon and the firmament, she abandoned without hesitation the pure atmosphere, to plunge into these infernal exhalations. The gait of those impious personages was haughty and determined. As they descended, by the effulgence of the torches, they gazed on each other with mutual admiration, and both appeared so resplendent, that they already esteemed themselves spiritual intelligences. The only circumstance that perplexed them, was their not arriving at the bottom of the stairs. On hastening their descent, with an ardent impetuosity, they felt their steps accelerated to such a degree, that they seemed not walking, but falling from a precipice. Their progress, however, was at length impeded by a vast portal of ebony, which the Caliph without difficulty recognized. Here the Giaour awaited them, with the key in his hand,

"Ye are welcome!" said he to them, with a ghastly smile, "in spite of Mahomet, and all his dependents. I will now admit you into that palace, where you have so highly merited a place."

Whilst he was uttering these words, he touched the enamelled lock with his key, and the doors at once expanded with a noise still louder than the thunder of mountains, and as suddenly recoiled the moment they had entered.

The Caliph and Nouronihar beheld each other with amazement, at finding themselves in a place which, though roofed with a vaulted ceiling, was so spacious and lofty, that at first they took it for an immeasurable plain. But their eyes at length growing to the grandeur of the objects at hand, they extended their view to those at a distance, and discovered rows of columns and arcades, which gradually diminished, till they terminated in a point, radiant as the sun, when he darts his last beams athwart the ocean. The pavement, strewed over with gold dust and saffron, exhaled so subtile an odour, as almost overpowered them. They, however, went on, and observed an infinity of censers, in which ambergris and the wood of aloes were continually burning. Between the several columns were placed tables, each spread with a profusion of viands, and wines of every species, sparkling in vases of chrystal. A throng of Genii, and other phantastic spirits, of each sex, danced lasciviously in troops, at the sound of music which issued from beneath.

In the midst of this immense hall, a vast multitude was incessantly passing, who severally kept their right hands on their hearts, without once regarding any thing around them. They had all the livid paleness of death. Their eyes, deep sank in their sockets, resembled those phosphoric meteors, that glimmer by night in places of interment. Some stalked slowly on, absorbed in profound reverie; some shrieking with agony, ran furiously about, like tigers wounded with poisoned arrows; whilst others, grinding their teeth in rage, foamed along, more frantic than the wildest maniac. They all avoided each other, and though surrounded by a multitude that no one could number, each wandered at random unheedful of the rest, as if alone on a desert which no foot had trodden.

Vathek and Nouronihar, frozen with terror at a sight so baleful, demanded of the Giaour what these appearances might mean, and why these ambulating spectres never withdrew their hands from their hearts.

"Perplex not yourselves," replied he bluntly, "with so much at once, you will soon be acquainted with all; let us haste and present you to Eblis."

They continued their way through the multitude, but notwithstanding their confidence at first, they were not sufficiently composed to examine with attention the various perspectives of halls, and of galleries, that opened on the right hand and left, which were all illuminated by torches and braziers, whose flames rose in pyramids, to the centre of the vault. At length they came to a place where long curtains, brocaded with crimson and gold, fell from all parts, in striking confusion. Here the choirs and dances were heard no longer. The light which glimmered came from afar.

After some time Vathek and Nouronihar perceived a gleam brightening through the drapery, and entered a vast tabernacle, carpeted with the skins of leopards. An infinity of elders, with streaming beards, and afrits, in complete armour, had prostrated themselves before the ascent of a lofty eminence, on the top of which, upon a globe of fire, sat the formidable Eblis. His person was that of a young man, whose noble and regular features seemed to have been tarnished by malignant vapours. In his large eyes appeared both pride and despair; his flowing hair retained some resemblance to that of an angel of light. In his hand, which thunder had blasted, he swayed the iron sceptre, that causes the monster Ouranabad,[26] the afrits, and all the powers of the abyss to tremble. At his presence the heart of the Caliph sank within him, and, for the first time, he fell prostrate on his face. Nouronihar, however, though greatly dismayed, could not help admiring the person of Eblis, for she expected to have seen some stupendous giant. Eblis, with a voice more mild than might be imagined, but such as transfused through the soul the deepest melancholy, said:

"CREATURES OF CLAY, I receive you into mine empire. Ye are numbered amongst my adorers. Enjoy whatever this palace affords—the treasures of the preadimite sultans, their bickering sabres, and those talismans that compel the Dives to open the subterranean expanses of the mountain of Kaf, which communicate with these. There, insatiable as your curiosity may be, shall you find sufficient to gratify it. You shall possess the exclusive privilege of entering the fortress of Aherman, and the halls of Argenk, where are portrayed all creatures endowed with intelligence, and the various animals that inhabited the earth prior to the creation of that contemptible being, whom ye denominate the Father of Mankind."

Vathek and Nouronihar feeling themselves revived and encouraged by this harangue, eagerly said to the Giaour:

"Bring us instantly to the place which contains these precious talismans."

"Come," answered this wicked Dive, with his malignant grin, "come, and possess all that my sovereign hath promised, and more."

He then conducted them into a long aisle adjoining the tabernacle, preceding them with hasty steps, and followed by his disciples with the utmost alacrity. They

---

[26] *Ouranabad*. This monster is represented as a fierce flying hydra, and belongs to the same class with the *Rakshe*, whose ordinary food was serpents and dragons; the *Soham*, which had the head of a horse, with four eyes, and the body of a flame-coloured dragon; the *Syl*, a basilisk with a face resembling the human, but so tremendous that no mortal could bear to behold it; the *Ejder*, and others. See these respective titles in Richardson's Dictionary, Persian, Arabic and English.

reached at length a hall of great extent, and covered with a lofty dome, around which appeared fifty portals of bronze, secured with as many fastenings of iron. A funereal gloom prevailed over the whole scene. Here, upon two beds of incorruptible cedar, lay recumbent the fleshless forms of the preadimite kings, who had been monarchs of the whole earth. They still possessed enough of life to be conscious of their deplorable condition. Their eyes retained a melancholy motion; they regarded each other with looks of the deepest dejection, each holding his right hand motionless on his heart. At their feet were inscribed the events of their several reigns, their power, their pride, and their crimes. Soliman Raad, Soliman Daki, and Soliman Di Gian Ben Gian, who, after having chained up the Dives in the dark caverns of Kaf, became so presumptuous, as to doubt of the Supreme Power. All these maintained great state, though not to be compared with the eminence of Soliman Ben Daoud.

This king, so renowned for his wisdom, was on the loftiest elevation, and placed immediately under the dome. He appeared to possess more animation than the rest, though, from time to time, he laboured with profound sighs, and, like his companions, kept his right hand on his heart; yet his countenance was more composed, and he seemed to be listening to the sullen roar of a vast cataract, visible in part through the grated portals. This was the only sound that intruded on the silence of these doleful mansions. A range of brazen vases surrounded the elevation.

"Remove the covers from these cabalistic depositaries," said the Giaour to Vathek, "and avail thyself of the talismans, which will break asunder all these gates of bronze, and not only render thee master of the treasures contained within them, but also of the spirits by which they are guarded."

The Caliph, whom this ominous preliminary had entirely disconcerted, approached the vases with faltering footsteps, and was ready to sink with terror, when he heard the groans of Soliman. As he proceeded, a voice from the livid lips of the prophet articulated these words:

"In my lifetime, I filled a magnificent throne, having on my right hand twelve thousand seats of gold, where the patriarchs and prophets heard my doctrines; on my left the sages and doctors, upon as many thrones of silver, were present at all my decisions. Whilst I thus administered justice to innumerable multitudes, the birds of the air librating over me, served as a canopy from the rays of the sun. My people flourished, and my palace rose to the clouds. I erected a temple to the Most High, which was the wonder of the universe; but I basely suffered myself to be seduced by the love of women, and a curiosity that could not be restrained by sub-lunary things. I listened to the counsels of Aherman, and the daughter of Pharaoh; and adored fire, and the host of heaven. I forsook the holy city, and commanded the Genii to rear the stupendous palace of Istakar, and the terrace of the watch-towers, each of which was consecrated to a star. There for a while I enjoyed myself in the zenith of glory and pleasure. Not only men, but supernatural existences were subject also to my will. I began to think, as these unhappy monarchs around had already thought, that the vengeance of heaven was asleep, when at once the thunder burst my structures asunder, and precipitated me hither; where, however, I do not remain like the other inhabitants totally destitute of hope, for an angel of light hath revealed, that in consideration of the piety of my early youth, my woes shall come to an end when this cataract shall for ever cease to flow. Till then I am in torments, ineffable torments, an unrelenting fire preys on my heart."

Having uttered this exclamation, Soliman raised his hands towards heaven, in token of supplication, and the Caliph discerned through his bosom, which was transparent as crystal, his heart enveloped in flames. At a sight so full of horror, Nouronihar fell back like one petrified, into the arms of Vathek, who cried out with a convulsive sob:

"O Giaour! whither hast thou brought us! Allow us to depart, and I will relinquish all thou hast promised. O Mahomet! remains there no more mercy!"

"None! none!" replied the malicious Dive. "Know, miserable prince, thou art now in the abode of vengeance, and despair. Thy heart, also, will be kindled, like those of the other votaries of Eblis. A few days are allotted thee previous to this fatal period: employ them as thou wilt. Recline on these heaps of gold: command the Infernal Potentates: range at thy pleasure through these immense subterranean domains. No barrier shall be shut against thee. As for me, I have fulfilled my mission. I now leave thee to thyself."

At these words he vanished.

The Caliph and Nouronihar remained in the most abject affliction. Their tears unable to flow, scarcely could they support themselves. At length, taking each other despondingly by the hand, they went faltering from this fatal hall, indifferent which way they turned their steps. Every portal opened at their approach. The Dives fell prostrate before them. Every reservoir of riches was disclosed to their view, but they no longer felt the incentives of curiosity, pride, or avarice. With like apathy they heard the chorus of Genii, and saw the stately banquets prepared to regale them. They went wandering on from chamber to chamber, hall to hall, and gallery to gallery; all without bounds or limit; all distinguishable by the same lowering gloom; all adorned with the same awful grandeur; all traversed by persons in search of repose and consolation, but who sought them in vain, for every one carried within him a heart tormented in flames. Shunned by these various sufferers, who seemed by their looks to be upbraiding the partners of their guilt, they withdrew from them, to wait in direful suspense the moment which should render them to each other the like objects of terror.

"What," exclaimed Nouronihar, "will the time come, when I shall snatch my hand from thine!"

"Ah!" said Vathek, "and shall my eyes ever cease to drink from thine long draughts of enjoyment! Shall the moments of our reciprocal ecstasies be reflected on with horror! It was not thou that broughtest me hither; the principles by which Carathis perverted my youth have been the sole cause of my perdition!"

Having given vent to these painful expressions, he called to an Afrit, who was stirring up one of the braziers, and bade him fetch the Princess Carathis from the palace of Samarah.

After issuing these orders, the Caliph and Nouronihar continued walking amidst the silent crowd, till they heard voices at the end of the gallery. Presuming them to proceed from some unhappy beings, who like themselves were awaiting their final doom, they followed the sound, and found it to come from a small square chamber, where they discovered sitting on sofas, five young men of goodly figure, and a lovely female, who were all holding a melancholy conversation, by the glimmering of a lonely lamp. Each had a gloomy and forlorn air, and two of them were embracing each other with great tenderness. On seeing the Caliph and the daughter of Fakreddin enter they arose, saluted, and gave them place. Then he who had appeared the most considerable of the group, addressed himself thus to Vathek:

"Strangers! who doubtless are in the same state of suspense as ourselves, as you do not yet bear your hand on your heart, if you are come hither to pass the interval allotted previous to the infliction of our common punishment, condescend to relate the adventures that have brought you to this fatal place; and we in return will acquaint you with ours; which deserves but too well to be heard. We will trace back our crimes to their source, though we are not permitted to repent. This is the only employment suited to wretches like us."

The Caliph and Nouronihar assented to the proposal, and Vathek began, not without tears and lamentations, a sincere recital of every circumstance that had passed. When the afflicting narrative was closed, the young man entered on his own. Each person proceeded in order, and when the fourth prince had reached the midst of his adventures, a sudden noise interrupted him, which caused the vault to tremble, and to open.

Immediately a cloud descended, which gradually dissipating, discovered Carathis, on the back of an Afrit, who grievously complained of his burden. She, instantly springing to the ground, advanced towards her son, and said:

"What dost thou here, in this little square chamber? As the Dives are become subject to thy beck, I expected to have found thee on the throne of the preadimite kings."

"Execrable woman!" answered the Caliph; "cursed be the day thou gavest me birth! Go! follow this Afrit; let him conduct thee to the hall of the Prophet Soliman; there thou wilt learn to what these palaces are destined, and how much I ought to abhor the impious knowledge thou hast taught me."

"The height of power to which thou art arrived, has certainly turned thy brain," answered Carathis; "but I ask no more, than permission to show my respect for the prophet. It is, however, proper thou shouldst know, that, as the Afrit has informed me neither of us shall return to Samarah, I requested his permission to arrange my affairs, and he politely consented. Availing myself, therefore, of the few moments allowed me, I set fire to the tower, and consumed in it the mutes, negresses, and serpents, which have rendered me so much good service; nor should I have been less kind to Morakanabad, had he not prevented me, by deserting at last to thy brother. As for Bababalouk, who had the folly to return to Samarah, and all the good brotherhood to provide husbands for thy wives, I undoubtedly would have put them to the torture, could I but have allowed them the time. Being, however, in a hurry, I only hung him, after having caught him in a snare with thy wives; whilst them I buried alive by the help of my negresses, who thus spent their last moments, greatly to their satisfaction. With respect to Dilara, who ever stood high in my favour, she hath evinced the greatness of her mind, by fixing herself near, in the service of one of the Magi, and, I think, will soon be our own."

Vathek, too much cast down to express the indignation excited by such a discourse, ordered the Afrit to remove Carathis from his presence, and continued immersed in thought, which his companions durst not disturb.

Carathis, however, eagerly entered the dome of Soliman, and, without regarding in the least the groans of the Prophet, undauntedly removed the covers of the vases, and violently seized on the talismans. Then, with a voice more loud than had hitherto been heard in these mansions, she compelled the Dives to disclose to her the most secret treasures, the most profound stores, which the Afrit himself had not seen. She passed by rapid descents known only to Eblis and his most favoured Potentates, and thus penetrated the very entrails of the earth, where breathes the Sansar, or icy wind of death. Nothing appalled her dauntless soul. She perceived, however, in all the inmates who bore their hands on their heart, a little singularity not much to her taste. As she was emerging from one of the abysses, Eblis stood forth to her view, but, notwithstanding he displayed the full effulgence of his infernal majesty, she preserved her countenance unaltered, and even paid her compliments with considerable firmness.

This superb monarch thus answered:

"PRINCESS, whose knowledge and whose crimes have merited a conspicuous rank in my empire, thou doest well to employ the leisure that remains, for the flames and torments which are ready to seize on thy heart, will not fail to provide thee with full employment."

He said this, and was lost in the curtains of his tabernacle.

Carathis paused for a moment with surprise, but, resolved to follow the advice of Eblis, she assembled all the choirs of Genii, and all the Dives, to pay her homage. Thus marched she in triumph through a vapour of perfumes, amidst the acclamations of all the malignant spirits; with most of whom she had formed a previous acquaintance. She even attempted to dethrone one of the Solimans, for the purpose of usurping his place, when a voice, proceeding from the Abyss of Death, proclaimed:

"All is accomplished!"

Instantaneously, the haughty forehead of the intrepid princess became corrugated with agony; she uttered a tremendous yell, and fixed—no more to be withdrawn—her right hand upon her heart, which was become a receptacle of eternal fire.

In this delirium, forgetting all ambitious projects, and her thirst for that knowledge which should ever be hidden from mortals, she overturned the offerings of the Genii; and, having execrated the hour she was begotten, and the womb that had borne her, glanced off in a whirl that rendered her invisible, and continued to revolve without intermission.

At almost the same instant, the same voice announced to the Caliph, Nouronihar, the five princes, and the princess, the awful and irrevocable decree. Their hearts immediately took fire, and they at once lost the most precious of the gifts of heaven—HOPE. These unhappy beings recoiled, with looks of the most furious distraction. Vathek beheld in the eyes of Nouronihar nothing but rage and vengeance; nor could she discern ought in his but aversion and despair. The two princes who were friends, and till that moment had preserved their attachment, shrunk back, gnashing their teeth with mutual and unchangeable hatred. Kalilah and his sister made reciprocal gestures of imprecation; whilst the two other princes testified their horror for each other by the most ghastly convulsions, and screams that could not be smothered. All severally plunged themselves into the accursed multitude, there to wander in an eternity of unabating anguish.

Such was, and such should be, the punishment of unrestrained passions, and atrocious actions. Such is, and such should be, the chastisement of blind ambition, that would transgress those bounds which the Creator hath prescribed to human knowledge, and by aiming at discoveries reserved for pure intelligence, acquire that infatuated pride, which perceives not the condition appointed to man is, TO BE IGNORANT AND HUMBLE.

Thus the CALIPH VATHEK who, for the sake of empty pomp and forbidden power, hath sullied himself with a thousand crimes, became a prey to grief without end, and remorse without mitigation; whilst the humble and despised GULCHENROUZ passed whole ages in undisturbed tranquillity, and the pure happiness of childhood.

Lector House believes that a society develops through a two-fold approach of continuous learning and adaptation, which is derived from the study of classic literary works spread across the historic timeline of literature records. Therefore, we aim at reviving, repairing and redeveloping all those inaccessible or damaged but historically as well as culturally important literature across subjects so that the future generations may have an opportunity to study and learn from past works to embark upon a journey of creating a better future.

This book is a result of an effort made by Lector House towards making a contribution to the preservation and repair of original ancient works which might hold historical significance to the approach of continuous learning across subjects.

HAPPY READING & LEARNING!

LECTOR HOUSE LLP
E-MAIL: lectorpublishing@gmail.com